Sherlock Holmes and the Bolshevik Plot

Eddie Maguire

First published in 2023 by
Baker Street Studios Ltd and
The Irregular Special Press for
Breese Books
Endeavour House
170 Woodland Road, Sawston
Cambridge, CB22 3DX, UK

Overall © Baker Street Studios Ltd, 2023

All rights reserved

No parts of this publication may be reproduced, stored in retrieval systems or transmitted in any form or by any means, electronic, mechanical, photocopying, recording or otherwise, except brief extracts for the purposes of review, without prior permission of the publishers.

Any paperback edition of this book, whether published simultaneously with, or subsequent to, the case bound edition, is sold subject to the condition that it shall not by way of trade, be lent, resold, hired out or otherwise disposed of without the publisher's consent, in any form of binding or cover other than that in which it was published.

This is a work of fiction. Names, characters, businesses, places, events and incidents are either the products of the author's imagination or used in a fictitious manner. Any resemblance to actual persons, living or dead, or actual events is purely coincidental.

ISBN: 978-1-901091-50-2

Cover Illustration: The deposed Tsar Nicholas II in the grounds of the imperial palace at Tsarskoye Selo where he was held with his wife and children after the February Revolution, 1917. In August he would be sent to Tobolsk in Siberia.

Typeset in 8/11/20pt Palatino

By the same author

Sherlock Holmes and the Tandridge Hall Murder
(includes A Death at the Cricket available as an audiobook)

Sherlock Holmes and the Secret Mission

Sherlock Holmes and the Highcliffe Invitation

Tsar Nicholas II with his wife, Tsaritsa Alexandra, in their full coronation regalia, May 1896.

Prologue

It was just after sunset and the departing sun had turned the cloud from white to coral pink. The Greek-owned ship carrying us to our destination cut through rippling, silver-tipped water, leaving a white frothy spume in her wake. Sherlock Holmes and I stood leaning on the rail, watching the swiftly departing shores of Italy where the lights of Brindisi twinkled in the growing darkness.

As I watched the lights recede and grow fainter all along the coast both to the north and to the south, I could see other lights being added to their luminescence and before very long the whole coast resembled a sparkling diamond necklace. I sighed and wondered how I had managed to find myself in this strange situation, sailing as I was into the complete unknown. Then I smiled as I recalled that it had all come about because of my decision to retire from general practice and rekindle my friendship with Sherlock Holmes.

I gazed at the man himself leaning on the rail deep in his own thoughts. How simple it had seemed that March morning when it had finally occurred to me that at three months into the new year of 1912 that I had been a medical practitioner for nearly thirty-five years and that it was a profession in which I no longer wished to serve. Sherlock Holmes had met me at the station and we travelled the seven miles to his cliff-top villa and all I was now considering was retirement, relaxation and perhaps a little beekeeping.

Together we explored the Sussex countryside and her shores and beaches but our idyll was shattered by the midnight visit of two of His Majesty's most trusted servants; a senior man at the Foreign Office and his military attaché. They brought with them information of a particularly delicate nature involving embryonic plans to unseat the Tsar of Russian. Europe, we were told, was nearly at crisis point with Britain, France and Russia eyeing Germany, Austria, Hungary and Serbia with particular suspicion. War had broken out in the Balkans and there was a very great risk that the rest of Europe might be dragged into the conflict.

In order to forestall any further deterioration in relations the great powers had called a conference, which was to meet soon in Rome, and His Majesty's Government had decided our representative should be none other than Holmes's brother, Mycroft. The elder Holmes, although a man of considerable intellect and experience in matters political, was somewhat advanced in years for such a sojourn, but it was felt that no other man in the land would be more fitted for the task.

Unfortunately Mycroft had fallen ill whilst in Rome and the gentlemen from the Foreign Office had come to see if the younger Holmes might be persuaded to take his place. Holmes, however, felt that this to be impossible so the matter was dropped.

Then, just a few days later, a letter containing crushing news arrived for my friend. Mycroft had succumbed to his illness and his mortal remains were now lying in the Bixio Clinic a short journey from Rome. Holmes was greatly affected by the death of his brother, and although he continued to act in a quite normal and business-like manner, his return to London upset a number of securely entrenched people, both high and low in status.

Everything, however, was not quite as it seemed to be for the medical report showed that Mycroft had fallen victim to a condition from which Holmes knew with certainty he could not have suffered. Clearly something was very wrong.

Then Holmes took it into his head that Mycroft was not dead and was almost certainly a prisoner of the authorities that ran the clinic; an act perhaps carried out on the instructions of an unfriendly power seeking to subvert the aims of the international conference. Holmes, therefore, decided that he would travel to Rome incognito and discover for himself the exact circumstances of the matter. He also asked if I would care to accompany him.
    Unfortunately a complication in the shape of Inspector Lestrade hindered our preparations. Hearing that Holmes was back in his old rooms, the detective had come to ask him for some advice about a strange kidnapping. Holmes was quick to turn this interview to his own advantage, however, for hearing that Lestrade knew all about his brother's death, proceeded to convince the detective that his sanity was at stake with a bravura performance which terrified Lestrade and frankly puzzled me.
    Afterwards, Holmes declared that his apparent descent into madness would provide us with excellent cover for our trip to Rome. If he could disappear into a clinic with me as his personal physician then he would be free to wander at will.
    Matters, however, became further complicated by the sudden arrival of Mrs. Andrews, the distraught wife of the kidnapped man Lestrade had talked about earlier. She desired Holmes to uncover the reason why her husband had been taken. He replied by explaining that he had retired, but relented when the lady broke down in tears. Then, as she explained the circumstances under which Mr. Andrews had been taken away, a chance discovery led Holmes to ordering the lady and myself back to her home in St. John's Wood.
    There we discovered that in her absence a curious burglary had taken place and whilst a good deal of confusion reigned, only Mr. Andrews's set of specialist tools had been taken. Upon further investigation, Holmes discovered that the two men who had taken Mr. Andrews had a Russian connection and that they had kidnapped him for an, as yet, unknown purpose.

Later Holmes and I were visited at our rooms by a sailor who had been the unfortunate victim of a violent attack. Whilst not in danger of his life he was very poorly, nevertheless. After treatment he was keen to tell Holmes a strange tale about how he had been witness to what appeared to be the product of a kidnapping when two men had brought a third aboard his ship. The ship, incidentally, was due to sail immediately for Naples.

Holmes now declared that we had a remarkable card to play, the sailor would be admitted to the clinic bearing the name of Sherlock Holmes, whilst he would be on his way to Italy in disguise. In response to my questioning Holmes revealed that once again he would be the elderly nonconformist cleric of years gone by whilst I should become a travelling salesman.

Our plans were a success; then when we were on the Milan-bound train from Paris, Holmes was called upon to assist a young English woman who had been accused of stealing a valuable piece of jewellery from her noble employers. Holmes solved the case with a very clever piece of subterfuge.

Once in Rome Holmes decided upon an immediate assault upon the Bixio Clinic where Mycroft was almost certainly being held captive. With the invaluable assistance of Milan Spasich, our guide to the centuries through which we were soon to pass, we set off at the dead of night and succeeded in entering the clinic and releasing Mycroft from his captivity. We escaped fleeing the burning building in a hail of bullets.

After an interview with the skipper of the boat carrying the kidnapped man from England, Holmes concluded that there was indeed a Russian connection, and that Andrews was being taken to St. Petersburg. However, there was insufficient information for him to say exactly why.

Holmes decided, therefore, that it was necessary for us to follow these fellows in order to find an opportunity to frustrate their plans. Then briefly it seemed that a journey would be unnecessary, but fate decreed that we should have to go.

I looked one last time at the coastline of Italy as it slowly receded and nodded to myself; all this, indeed, had come about because of my desire to renew my friendship with Sherlock Holmes. As to what the future might bring I could not say. I only felt certain of one thing. If it involved Sherlock Holmes, then it would inevitably prove to be stimulating!

Barely three hours before, we had said our goodbyes to His Majesty's Ambassador, General Wilton who, despite his strongly vocalised opinion that we were both stark staring mad, had come down to the quay side to bid us bon voyage.

Sherlock Holmes had thoroughly prepared for our journey to St. Petersburg. The trail he had mapped out would take us through the Balkans, Montenegro and Serbia, Roumania and then Ukranian Russia and Russia proper to the city of St. Peter the Great. Holmes explained that this was undoubtedly the route taken by the Russians and, in answer to my query why they should take such an inordinately circuitous course, Holmes explained, "These men are agents of an exiled Russian agitator and are unable to travel freely in Europe. Certainly, the more direct route to St. Petersburg, through Austro-Hungarian and German territory, would be quicker but it would be fraught with dangers. So this particular route through Slav states remains their only avenue."

I looked doubtfully at Holmes, "But why do we not travel directly to St. Petersburg and wait upon their arrival instead of roaming across backward and harsh lands in pursuit of someone with whom we may never catch up?"

"Ah, but we may," said Holmes emphatically. "As you rightly say, the journey will be rough and uncomfortable, but it is the same for our quarry. They may come to grief. As the old proverb says there is many a slip, twixt cup and lip."

"Hmm," I mused. "That is as maybe, Holmes, but it occurs to me, the same misfortunes may befall us."

Holmes smiled. "We are at least twenty-four hours behind our quarry. If fortune favours us, we shall arrive at our destination at no less a disadvantage. In St. Petersburg we will have up to four days grace, whilst our friends report to their employer and await either his reply or, if we are fortunate, his personal appearance. During that time we may frustrate their plans."

I smiled wanly at my companion. "Let us trust you are right, Holmes. Then we may rescue Hunter Andrews from the fate they have prepared for him."

Holmes nodded his assent. "Indeed, but remember this, Watson. There is something far greater at stake here, unless I miss my guess, we are pursuing those who are involved in a plot, which if successful, will shake the Eagle thrones of Europe to their very foundations."

Somewhat stunned and mystified by his cool revelation, I blurted out, "Holmes, you are virtually intimating that the very future of Europe may hang upon the success or failure of our mission?"

Holmes looked at me grimly, his eyes glowing in the last vestige of twilight. Yet his voice was soft, even soothing. "That it may, Doctor. That it may."

It is quite rightly said that seamen are a hardy race. Of that there is no doubt, but if our culinary experience aboard the tramp steamer to Montenegro was typical of the food served up to them, then their stomachs are even hardier. To describe the cuisine as basic is something of an understatement. Fortunately, however, we were due to remain on board for under a day, so it was an inconvenience with which we felt ourselves able to put up.

The ship, a large ancient coke-fired leviathan, chugged along in the velvety darkness. Our progress was slow and stately and it would be only a little before dawn when we made landfall.

Holmes, after a last turn upon deck, had taken to his bunk. Milan and I, meanwhile played a few hands of cards. "Dr. Watson," Milan said suddenly. "Why do you do this thing?"

Slightly startled by his sudden question, I replied rather sharply. "Does it surprise you that two Englishmen are trying to succour a fellow countryman?"

"No, indeed," he smiled. "But to cross half a continent in pursuit of someone you may fail to help in the end, it seems just a little fantastic, no?"

"Well, if you understood Sherlock Holmes as intimately as I, it would not surprise you so. His commitment to the cause is total. Hunter Andrews; and indeed his wife, need our assistance, therefore, they shall have it."

Milan still appeared troubled, however. "Quite so, Doctor. Mr. Holmes is pursuing his goals, I understand fully. But you have yet to explain why you follow him."

"Whither goest Holmes goest I."

Milan laughed. "Such loyalty to a friend and the course he chooses to pursue. These are the traits we here in the Balkans hold most highly. Why, Dr. Watson, you could almost be a Slav."

It was my turn to laugh. "Well, Englishman or Slav, we need our sleep. We have much to do in the morning, so let us to bed."

The coronation procession of Nicholas II makes its way through the streets of Moscow

One

A grey and foggy dawn was breaking, as we landed on the grey rocky shores of Montenegro.

Our transport was some time in arriving, so Holmes and I questioned Milan about the history of the area. Milan sat on a pile of brushwood and lit his pipe.

"You ask me to tell you something of the history of my region. Where do I begin? Perhaps I should first explain the history of the Balkans. Unlike other parts of Europe, which have long been settled by one people, the Balkans have been invaded by a variety of peoples. Look around you, Doctor, you will see Greek temples, Roman baths, a Byzantine church, several mosques and perhaps a Frankish castle. All this has come about because of our situation and the fact we are not protected by mountain ranges."

Milan took a stick from the pile he was sitting on and drew a map in the sand. "Unlike Spain or Italy, the Balkan Peninsula has no northern wall to shelter it from the rest of Europe. In place of the Alps and the Pyrenees, there is the wide Danube plain, which serves as a highway, rather than as a barrier."

He pointed to various areas, which roughly represented the countries surrounding the Balkans. "We are a mere fifty miles from Italy, Crete is a close stepping stone from Greece, and Asia Minor is just across the Bosphorus. Is it any wonder our lands have for so long been the battleground of peoples, cultures and religions?"

Sherlock Holmes slid from his rocky seat and walked around the roughly drawn map. "But this is a terribly mountainous region. It has to be wondered why such an unproductive area should be the target of so many alien forces." He squatted down and dropped several stones onto the map. "But perhaps it is the quantity of land that the empire builder concerns himself with and not the quality."

Milan smiled. "You are exactly right, Mr. Holmes. An empire builder does not concern himself about the value of the land. He is only concerned about how much of it he can grab. Only later does he consider the nature of the new province."

I considered the matter for a few moments. "Why have the indigenous people not banded together and repulsed the invaders?"

Milan shook his stick at the map and smiled grimly. "Mr. Holmes put his finger on the reason, Dr. Watson. It is because of the very topography of the region. It has meant the fragmentation of the population. Nowhere is there a natural centre around which a great state might crystallise. Indeed, unity has never come from within. It has been forced upon us from the outside."

Then from out of the gloom there came the sound of hooves. Moments later a closed carriage appeared. Milan jumped to his feet. "Maxim has come," he said, his voice betraying the relief he clearly felt. "Doctor, may I trouble you to assist me in erasing the map?"

As we rattled along the bumpy lanes, which led to Cetinji, Milan continued his potted history of the Balkans. He described the nature of the peoples inhabiting the region. "The most numerous are the South Slavs. To the North are the Slovenes, to the middle and the South West are the Croats, and in the middle and to the East are the Serbs, of which I am one.

"Further south and east are the Bulgars, the Macedonians and the Greeks. The remaining south-western area is inhabited by the Albanians."

I asked, "What of the Turk, for how long has he dominated the area?"

A look of ill-concealed disgust spread across Milan's face at the mention of the Turks. "From the middle of the fifteenth century the Turks held sway over nearly all the area. In 1804, my people rose in revolt and by 1807 had taken Beograde (You know it as Belgrade) from the Turks, but events elsewhere and beyond their control, allowed the Turks to regroup. In 1813, with Russia, our protector, locked in mortal combat with Napoleon, they renewed hostilities and retook the city.

"The Turks then began a reign of terror, and such was the magnitude of the Turkish revenge, that revolt broke out. On this occasion the patriots were led by Milosh Obrenovich. Under his command the Serbs forced the Turks into an acceptance of Serbian independence, and she should become on autonomous principality. For the moment the people were satisfied with this arrangement."

"A case of half a loaf being better than none," I said.

Milan nodded. He pulled back the curtain and peered outside. The fog seemed hardly to have lifted at all. "We are almost half way to the town he said. Perhaps there will be just enough time to finish my little history lesson."

Holmes felt in his pockets and produced his pipe.

"The Turks, I perceive, were finding the whole business of running an empire a little too rich for their blood. As I remember from my school history lessons, it was in the mid-1800s they lost control of Romania and much of Greece and Bulgaria," he said.

"Yes," agreed Milan. "The empire was crumbling and Russia seeing how the wind was blowing, declared war on Turkey and by March 1878 Turkey, had capitulated."

"What effect did this outcome have on the peoples of the Balkans?" I said.

"Serbia and Montenegro were to become fully independent states. Bulgaria was to be an independent principality. Romania was to be independent, but allied to Turkey, Bosnia Hertzogovina would be temporarily administered by Austria because there was no clear division of power among the inhabitants. Many were Serbs, some were Croats and a large number were Moslem converts.

"Then, in 1908, something of a revolution took place in the heart of the Turkish Empire. A group of army officers led by Mustapha Kamal staged a revolt and demanded that democracy laws passed in 1876 and subsequently ignored for over thirty years, be re-invoked. The Pasha was forced to agree. One of the consequences was the imposition of Turkish citizenship on all subject peoples. This was greeted with derision by the people of the Balkans."

"Perhaps if the Turks had adopted a more European cohesive empire in which the subjected peoples were afforded better treatment, possibly an arrangement could have been arrived at," I said.

"Yes," said Holmes languidly. "Possibly they could have arranged their empire in the fashion of the Belgians."

Holmes can be so boring when he is being sarcastic. Milan took out his watch, scanned it keenly and made a satisfied noise.

"It is nearly seven. We shall be in Cetinji before very long. So for the last part of the journey, we shall have the last part of my story," he said. "The democratisation of the Turkish empire was seen by its subject peoples not only as a sign of weakness, but also as an opportunity for one of the 'great powers' to take an advantage.

"Austria annexed Bosnia and Hertzagovina. This act of aggression outraged my people in Serbia, who for many years had been working towards a Balkan league of Slavic nations. She protested, but Austria was immovable. But because Russia felt unable to support her, Serbia could do nothing.

"The Balkan league, however, was founded in the spring of last year, its first act was to lobby Russia to assist them in their aim of releasing Bosnia and Hertzogovina from the clutches of the Hapsburgs.

"But in October, the scene changed. From north to south, Turkey had slackened her grip on the Balkans, because she had been fighting Italy over ports of North Africa.

"Several of the states saw the opportunity to try and force Turkey once and for all out of the Balkans. Accordingly Montenegro, Bulgaria, Greece and Serbia declared war on her. Turkey was forced to retreat on all sides, and by December sought an armistice. Agreement, however, was never reached and hostilities recommenced. As I speak, there is still fighting along the southern coasts, but Albania has been all but freed from the Turkish yoke. Now most of the Balkans has been cleared." Milan looked darkly at us and set his jaw. "All that now remains is the removal of Austria."

The carriage rattled onto the streets of Cetinji and very soon we stood before the gates of the ancient citadel. I looked up at the massive stone walls and observed the mixture of styles which had gone into its construction. Right at the very top, like a weathervane, was a broken crescent, the symbol of Turkey and also the symbol of her decline and fall.

Sherlock Holmes tapped the massive walls with his stick and gazed up at the monument of empire. "Will the Balkans ever be free of empires?" he wondered.

Milan looked darkly at him. "Have no doubt, Mr. Holmes, whatever the cost, the Balkans will be free."

*****

Suddenly a small panel in the gate slid open and a dark moustached face peered out. Clearly our conversation had been overheard. Milan held up his left hand and splayed his fingers. The panel shut with a bang. There came the sound of a lock being turned and the door swung slowly open, its ancient hinges creaking in protest. The opening was immediately filled by a large figure who looked doubtfully at us. Milan sprang forward, his hand extended.

"Spasich ... Negro," he said.

Suddenly the doorkeeper was all smiles. He gestured for us to enter. The two Slavs conversed for a few moments, then Milan turned back to Holmes and myself. "This is Darko. He is the town warden of Cetinji. You must forgive him his suspicion, but the people here are still wary of Turkish spies. I have told him you are "Inglich", so all is well."

Darko led us through a low gloomy gatehouse, then we entered into the light once more. Even at this relatively early hour the streets were busy with townspeople going about their daily business. To our western eyes they seemed strange and unfamiliar. What they must have made of our western garb and foreign tongue is a matter for conjecture, for many stopped and stared at us as we passed them by.

Our guide halted outside a large stone-clad building. He banged the great cast iron knocker with vigour.

"This is the house of Dr. Krasich, the mayor of Cetinji," Milan informed us. "He is the fellow to whom I wrote on your behalf when you informed me of your plans, Mr. Holmes. With any luck my message has reached him before we have."

The door was flung open and a tall, rather portly man stood there. Dr. Krasich, for it was he, gave a cry of joy and warmly embraced Milan. For a few moments the two men conversed in their own language, then the doctor addressed us in excellent English.

"Mr. Holmes, Dr. Watson, welcome, welcome. Milan's letter arrived only last night, so I have unfortunately been unable to make arrangements for your visit." He gave us a look of embarrassment and slapped his face. "But where are my manners? Please come in and take some refreshment."

After breakfast we retired to the Doctor's study, a spacious room overlooking a large courtyard, for a pipe and more coffee. Krasich asked us about our plans, but when Holmes outlined our proposed route, he pulled a face.

"The Balkans are a difficult place to travel through, Mr. Holmes. The people are extremely suspicious of outsiders. Milan has already spoken of the considerable interest engendered by your appearance this morning. I'm afraid that you stand out from the crowd too much and you will find that, unfortunately, your passage through the region will be constantly interrupted by petty officials questioning you about your movements."

"Oh, indeed," said Holmes. "I had anticipated as much and had determined to find suitable replacements for our western garb as quickly as possible. Perhaps you can assist us in the matter."

Krasich ran a quick eye over Holmes and myself. He smiled and patted his ample stomach. "Unfortunately, I have nothing suitable for you in my wardrobe, but perhaps I can send your details to my friend, Saskan, the tailor."

The Doctor laid down his pipe. "Now, gentlemen, what of your papers?"

Holmes took the letters of transit out from his pocket and handed them to our host. The Doctor examined them for a few moments. He looked back at Holmes, his face was grim. "This is no good. You must have papers in our language. Otherwise you will get precisely nowhere in the Balkans."

My heart sank. I looked at Holmes, his face bore a severe expression. "We are on an errand which may have international ramifications. We cannot afford to be held up. Tell me, Dr. Krasich, is there some way in which we may cut this Gordian knot?"

The Doctor knitted his brows together in thought and puffed vigorously on his pipe, sending clouds of smoke high into the air. Suddenly, he banged his fist on the table, sending a tremor through the contents. "The church's seal. You will need the church's seal."

Somewhat startled by his outburst, I cried. "What do you mean, Doctor? How can the church help us in this matter?"

Krasich smiled serenely at me. "There is a custom in our region which insists that anyone carrying a letter with the seal of the holy Orthodox Church is inviolate. No official will dare to impede you."

"Excellent," said Holmes. "But I perceive, however, that no local priest will be of sufficient importance to provide such a vehicle."

Krasich stood up and reached out for a spill to re-light his pipe and chuckled.

"Oh, indeed, Mr. Holmes. We can do much better than the local priest. Some ten miles away is the Monastir Moraca. The Prelate, Father Grigory, is an old friend of mine. We shall pay him a visit and ask for his help."

It was a little after noon when our partly left for the monastery. The carriage containing Holmes, Dr. Krasich, Milan and myself, was driven, as before, by the silent Maxim. Krasich had said that our journey was to be one of some ten miles and I had, in all innocence, imaging that we would arrive at our destination in under an hour. I was disappointed, however, to discover that after two hours we had travelled scarcely half the distance to the monastery. I glanced at Holmes, who was gazing idly out of the window at the rough and rocky terrain. How like Afghanistan the region was, and like Afghanistan how difficult travelling must be.

At length the carriage came to a halt. The road seemed simply to have petered out. Maxim, it appeared, had driven us into a *cul de sac*. To the left, I could see the land falling sharply away into a deep tree-lined gorge. To the right, a grey rocky cliff face rose at a sharp angle. Before us the road became a mere track, which was quickly lost behind a mass of bushes and stunted trees.

It suddenly occurred to me that this place was ideally situated for a trap. Had we been lured to this desolate spot to be subjected to robbery and who knows what? I felt in my pocket for my trusty service revolver. My stomach sank as I discovered it was not there. Indeed, as I had earlier changed into clothing more suitable for travelling through the area, I discovered that the pocket was no longer there. Too late, I realised that if there were to be trouble, my wits and not my weapon would be called into action.

Dr. Krasich, however, appeared quite unconcerned. He opened the carriage door and climbed down. "Come along, gentlemen. We walk from here."

Relieved that apparently we were not about to be ambushed, I followed the Doctor into the roadway. "But where are we?" I asked.

"At the monastery," he replied, pointing at the huge expanse of rock to our right. "If you look up there, Dr. Watson, you will see it."

For a moment I looked up. There at the very top, on the highest escarpment stood the huge ancient walls of the

Monastir Moraca, its golden spires gleaming in the afternoon sun.

Holmes looked at me and smiled at my obvious astonishment. "Mother church has been built on high to be closer to heaven, eh, Watson?"

"The house of God has been the fortress against the infidel," said Milan. "The Turkish scum could never hold sway here."

We followed the pathway around the foot of the cliff. Then we found ourselves at the edge of a smallholding with vegetables growing in abundance and fruit canes, cut and prepared for the coming summer. Several monks were hard at work and it was some little time before we could bring ourselves to their attention. Then one, a young man with a short beard, noticed our presence. He waved and came toward us, wiping his hands on a piece of cloth produced from the folds of his tunic. Recognising Krasich, he greeted him warmly. The Doctor turned to us. "Please follow me, gentlemen. Brother Antony tells me that father Grigory is in the library, and without doubt, will be pleased to see us."

The entrance to the monastery was achieved through three flights of stone steps carved into the cliff face. Holmes and Milan traversed them with consummate ease. As for Krasich and myself, the experience was somewhat less comfortable.

Brother Antony led us through the entrance gate and into the monastery courtyard. Before us stood an array of wooden buildings, mostly with thatched roofs, but imposing itself upon the whole estate, stood a massive stone-built tower tipped by the golden onion-dome and spires I had earlier observed. We were led up six steps and through two huge ornately carved doors and up yet another flight of stairs. Brother Antony finally led us into the *scriptorum*, a long whitewashed room lined with high arched windows glazed with a mixture of plain and frosted glass. Along the floor there stood three rows of high desks and stools and seated at several of the desks were a number of young monks deeply engrossed in the large volumes which lay before them. As I followed our guide I could see that these were ancient, beautifully inscribed bibles and that the monks were faithfully reproducing them by hand.

A door at the far end of the room opened and a generously bearded man dressed entirely in black appeared. It was Father Grigory.

"Father," said Krasich in French. "It is good to see you again. I have brought some friends who need your assistance. Mr. Sherlock Holmes, Dr. Watson and my old friend Milan Spasich."

"Good day, gentlemen. Welcome to God's house." He shook hands with Holmes and myself. "What is the nature of the problem which brings you so far from Baker Street?"

"Our names are familiar to you, Father?" I said.

"Indeed, Dr. Watson, was in France during the year of 1889. After your success in the matter of the *Hound of the Baskervilles*, your names were on everyone's lips. Although I may not be the first, I confidently expect to be the last to congratulate you."

Holmes bowed in acknowledgement and smiled briefly.

"Now, Mr. Holmes," said the priest, rubbing his hands together briskly. "How exactly may I help you?" Briefly Holmes explained our mission. The priest looked at us with astonishment.

"Your mission involves the Tsar of Russia. I can hardly believe it."

Sherlock Holmes gazed steadily at our host. "Believe it, sir. Whilst we are seeking the whereabouts of Hunter Andrews, it is my belief that his fate is inextricably bound up with that of Tsar Nicholas. If you are not prepared to assist us, please inform us now and we shall immediately turn around and return to England, leaving both Mr. Andrews and the Tsar to their fate."

Father Grigory's eyes widened a little, he appeared to be somewhat taken aback by the candid language of Sherlock Holmes. "Dear me, Mr. Holmes," he said. "I would not dream of seeking to hinder your errand. If you will please follow me to my chamber, I shall immediately draft a letter of passage for you; and if Dr. Krasich would care to accompany you, he may advise me on the exact contents."

For the short while in which Holmes and Krasich were closeted with the priest, Milan and I used our time in observing the scribes as they worked at their desks.

A little later Sherlock Holmes rejoined us. In his hand was a letter which bore the seal of the monastery. "There we are, my boy," he said cheerfully. "It is even better than anticipated. In my hand is a personal letter to the Patriarch of Kiev, who is an old friend of Father Grigory. It contains all the details relevant to our mission and a request that he should do all that is in his power to assist us."

The day had grown old by the time our carriage once more rattled on to the cobbled streets of Cetinji. Clearly we would travel no further this day. I comforted myself in the knowledge that we would enjoy two more decent meals before setting off on our arduous journey. Holmes, however, was less sanguine. "This is not good, Watson. We have already wasted a day. Now we are faced with a wasted night," he sighed. "I perceive, however, that we must make the best of a bad lot."

*****

It was a little after seven a.m. when Holmes, Milan and I stepped once more on to the streets of Cetinji. The early morning sun shone brightly from a pale blue sky, lighting up the snow-capped mountains surrounding the plain in which the town stood.

Holmes looked around and briskly rubbed his hands together. Like Milan and myself, he was warmly dressed against the cold early spring temperatures common to the region in which we found ourselves. "A fine crisp morning, eh, Watson?" he said.

Dr. Krasich appeared from a side entrance. He was leading three sturdy horses, strong limbed and still in their coats, yet mild and docile (I sincerely hoped!). It had been several years since my last regular ride and as a consequence, I was somewhat apprehensive about my present competence.

Clearly reading my mind, Holmes chuckled. "Do not worry, Doctor. You will soon find your seat. Riding is a skill one never loses."

"Indeed," I murmured. "Let us hope so."

Milan swung himself easily into the saddle of his chosen animal. "Do not worry, Dr. Watson, our destination of Bejelo Polje is under two days" distance. Then you may enjoy the comfort of our railways."

As I gingerly mounted my horse, I became aware of a rumbling noise coming from somewhere in the distance, which steadily grew louder. Then, from around the corner there appeared a large, black enclosed carriage, pulled by four horses with white plumes. As the carriage drew up along side the house I noticed that on the door there was a golden monogram. Dr. Krasich sighed audibly. I turned in my seat and looked at the Doctor. He appeared to have visibly paled. "It is Bogachevich," he said weakly. "The wolf has left his lair."

The carriage drew to a halt and the driver, a large dark-haired man, jumped down. He reached under the seat and drew out a wooden box and placed it on the ground. The door swung open and a large, hooked-nosed man with a perfect mane of white hair stepped down. He was quickly followed by two other bearded men dressed in sheepskin and leather.

"Krasich," the man spoke in a harsh voice but in surprisingly good English. "You are letting your guests depart without introduction to me. This will not do." He turned and looked keenly at us. "Mr. Holmes, Dr. Watson, you are most welcome in Montenegro." He looked at Milan with deeply unfriendly eyes. "Spasich, I never hoped to meet you again so soon and in such elevated company," he laughed. "You are coming up in the world, no?"

Milan returned Bogachevich's gaze with a sharp look which betrayed contempt. Clearly there existed some old enmity between the two men. For the present, however, Milan remained silent.

"Now, Mr. Holmes, Dr. Watson, please step down from your horses and let us talk for a while," said Bogachevich smiling.

"Thank you for your kind invitation, sir," Holmes replied. "But we are keen to be on our way. We have a long journey before us and an appointment to keep."

Bogachevich smiled again. He snapped his fingers and the sheepskin-clad men opened their coats and revealed the butts of two large guns. "You misunderstand me, Mr. Holmes. It was an order I issued, and not a request. Please step down."

I quickly looked across at Sherlock Holmes who signalled that I should obey.

"Now, gentlemen," said Bogachevich, his smile, if anything, broader than ever. "Dr. Krasich will take us to his house where we may talk." He linked arms with the Doctor and proceeded to lead Holmes, Milan and myself up the steps and once more into the house of Dr. Krasich.

I turned and spoke to Milan. "Who is this fellow Bogachevich?" I whispered.

Milan grimaced. "He is a villian," he growled. "He is a warlord, one of the many who sprang up during the time when we were fighting the Turks. He has recently become a *bone fide* politician in Serbia and is now a rich man. As you see, he surrounds himself with bodyguards who protect him as he extends his influence."

"You do not like him?"

"He is no friend to me, Dr. Watson. Oh, we once fought on the same side, but it was long ago. Long before he became corrupted by power."

Our conversation was rudely interrupted by a violent push in the back of Milan by one of the bodyguards. Milan shaped as if to strike him, but I swiftly restrained him from his rashness.

We assembled once more in the kitchen of Dr. Krasich. Mrs. Krasich appeared briefly at the door, her eyes widened at the sight of the warlord and she quickly vanished.

Bogachevich sat at the head of the table and signalled for us to sit down. "Now, Mr. Holmes. I believe you are on an urgent mission."

Holmes stared coldly at the Serb. "My business is my business," he said flatly.

Bogachevich laughed uproariously. "Mr. Holmes, Mr. Holmes, you are a man after my own heart. Indeed you are, sir."

"What do you want from us?" Holmes asked him.

"If you are to prosper in Montenegro and Serbia you will need papers, Mr. Holmes. I can supply these papers."

"But we have papers," I objected. "Only yesterday Father Grigory from the monastery provided us with the necessary letters of transit complete with the seal of the Orthodox Church."

Bogachevich once more exploded with laughter. "Oh, Dr. Watson," he said wiping away the tears from his eyes. "You really are priceless."

Then in a flash his demeanour changed from jovial to aggressive.

"The Church!" he cried. "What do I care for the Church?" He glared at Sherlock Holmes. "It is up to me whether you travel freely through this region. Your precious letter from Father Grigory means nothing to my associates or me. Understand this much, it is through my good offices, and none other, that you will travel freely through Montenegro and Serbia."

Sherlock Holmes gazed steadily at the warlord. He alone of our party seemed completely unperturbed. "Very well, sir. You want something from us. Will you give it a name? Then we may be on our way."

For the first time, Bogachevich seemed somewhat taken aback by the coolness of Sherlock Holmes. He looked at my friend and smiled thinly. "It is as you say, Mr. Holmes. So let me put a proposal to you. Your need is for papers, which will let you safely, pass through this region. As for myself … well, now; a man in my position needs finance. He smiled, feigning slight embarrassment it appeared. "Now, if we can come to some ... arrangement for your purchase of the papers. Then you may travel unhindered."

Holmes took out the small wad of currency notes given to him by General Wilton and held them out, but Bogachevich shook his head.

"Oh, no, Mr. Holmes. Money is not of much use for my circumstances. Do you not have something more ... negotiable? You have gold perhaps?"

Milan stood up and pointed an angry finger at Bogachevich. "Villian! Cur!" he screamed. "These are good and decent people, keep your filthy claws off them!" He threw aside his chair and launched into a stream of invective in their own language, which brought an angry flush to the cheeks of the warlord.

At a sign from Bogachevich, Milan was roughly grabbed by two of his bodyguards and thrown back into his chair.

Again, Holmes held up his hands in a gesture of conciliation. "My dear, sir, let us complete this transaction without further unpleasantness and be on our way," he reached into an inside pocket and produced his gold cigarette case which he laid upon the table. He took off his signet ring and set it alongside the case.

Bogachevich's eyes lit up with greed and avarice at the sight of so much gold.

Holmes turned to me, "Watson, I believe we are in need of one final item to pay our passage."

I looked blankly at my friend. "But I have nothing of value to contribute."

"You have your watch."

"My watch?" I cried in some surprise. "Surely, Holmes, you cannot mean me to give up my only family heirloom?"

"I am sorry, old fellow. But unless you give it up we shall go no further. There really is too much at stake to baulk at the loss of your watch."

I sighed deeply and felt into my inside pocket. Holmes, of course, was exactly right, but it was with a heavy heart I handed over my late brother's watch. Holmes pushed the precious objects across the table. Bogachevich picked them up with trembling fingers. "This is most acceptable, Mr. Holmes. You strike a good deal. For this I will even forget the hard words of Spasich."

He reached into an inside pocket and produced a long white envelope. From this envelope, he extracted a folded sheet of paper, and handed it to Dr. Krasich.

The Doctor quickly read the paper and handed it back to Bogachevich who took out from his top pocket a large gold fountain pen and proceeded to sign it with a flourish. He then refolded the paper and handed it to Holmes.

"As Dr. Krasich will confirm, Mr. Holmes, this letter guarantees your unrestricted access to any part of Serbia you may wish to travel to."

I looked across to Krasich who nodded his assent.

"There gentlemen, you may go." Bogachevich stood up and signalled to his henchmen. The larger of the two sprang to attention as his master strode past him. As the warlord drew level with Milan he gave him a hard stare. "It is as well, Spasich, that you are in the service of someone to whom I have granted safe passage. But do not come this way again. On another occasion I may not be so understanding."

As Bogachevich reached the doorway Sherlock Holmes approached him, his hand held out. "Goodbye, sir. It is not often I am bested, let me congratulate you, therefore."

The Serb took his hand and slapped Holmes heartily on the back. He laughed loudly.

"You are a good man, Mr. Holmes, but in the Balkans you are out of your league," he said. "Good luck in your travels, I hope you get your man."

Then he was gone. The front door closed with a bang and there came the rumble of the heavy carriage once more as the warlord and his minions departed. There was a long silence in the room. Dr. Krasich was the first to break the stillness.

"Gentlemen," he said quietly. "I am so sorry. I had no idea that … that villain was near to hand. That paper Bogachevich has signed is perfectly worthless. He can revoke it at a moment's notice. You have given up your gold for nothing."

Milan thumped the table angrily. "That man is a swine; a dog; a rat. He is life unworthy of life!"

For myself I was speechless with grief and shame. Holmes, seeing my dejection, walked around the table and patted me gently on the shoulder. "My dear, fellow. What must you think of me? My only excuse is that fellow was playing a game of his own devising with a marked deck of cards, and all the aces in his hand."

I looked up at Holmes and sighed deeply. "You really had no option but to dance to the rascal's tune," I said bravely.

"Good old, Watson, loyal to the last."

He smiled and sat down beside me. "I believe, however, that I held one card with which I could outplay Bogachevich. Do you wish to see this trump card, Watson?"

"Indeed, I would," I replied much mystified.

Holmes felt into his jacket pocket and to my complete surprise and delight, produced a gold cigarette case, a gold signet ring and, to my overwhelming joy, my brother's watch. "The Ace of Spades, eh, Watson?"

"My dear fellow," I cried. "This is wonderful. How on Earth did you do it?"

Holmes waved his hands in a casual manner. "Oh, just a little pick-pocketing when I made my farewells. I am no wolf, Watson, but perhaps I may be a fox."

Milan, roaring with laughter dragged Holmes from his chair and seized him in a bear hug. Laughing loudly, Dr. Krasich and I shook hands. Mrs. Krasich once more appeared in the doorway, her eyes as large as saucers. She appeared to think we had all gone quite mad.

Sherlock Holmes disentangled himself from Milan's grip and banged the table with a large serving spoon. He held up his hand for silence.

"Gentlemen, my trump card may yet turn into the death card. Sooner or later Bogachevich will discover his loss. He will doubtless spend some time searching for his treasures, but it will not be long before he comprehends what has occurred and returns here seeking revenge. I do not wish to be here and suffer his ire, so, Dr. Krasich, if you will kindly help us with our packs, and point us in the direction of Bejelo Polje, we shall swiftly take our leave."

*****

Our little party of travellers spent the best part of the next two days on horseback and as a consequence a certain part of my anatomy was crying out for relief. At the journey's outset, Holmes had calculated us to be almost twenty-four hours behind our quarry. The delay induced by our visit to Monstir Moraca and the subsequent meeting with Mr. Bogachevich had served to increase their advantage to almost two days. Whilst it was true that, supposing we suffered no further impediment, we would still have two free days in St. Petersburg, so with any luck we would round them up before they could complete their mission.

Our packs by now had become decidedly light. The provisions thoughtfully provided by Dr. Krasich were almost exhausted, but on the second morning we were fortunate enough to come across a friendly farmer on his way back from his fields and he provided us with onions, eggs, freshly baked bread and some cheese. So it was at noon, we made camp in a small copse of gnarled and stunted trees.

Holmes produced his pipe and leaned back against one of the trees. He stretched his legs out before him and sighed contentedly. "The simple life, eh, Watson?" He took a pull at his pipe and blew a smoke ring into the air. "I believe that under more auspicious circumstances, our sojourn would be rather pleasant."

"Although my brain agrees with you, Holmes," I said frowning "there is another part of my anatomy which disputes profoundly with your sentiments."

The sound of horse's hooves suddenly interrupted our reverie. Holmes sprang to his feet and signalled to Milan that he should extinguish the fire. I felt for my revolver.

Holmes indicated to Milan that he should watch the road and to me that I should go to the horses. Cupping his hands to his lips, he whispered, "watch the horses and ensure that they do not become alarmed and betray us."

As I patted and stroked the horses, I noticed a rider, moving slowly along the rocky path to the rear of the copse. Scarcely daring to draw breath, I watched as his horse carefully picked its way along the track and I could hardly believe my luck when at last the rider moved out of sight once more. Fortunately it was the road before him and not the countryside that surrounded him which had occupied his attention.

I drew a deep breath. There was a slight rustle from behind which made me jump. I spun around to discover Sherlock Holmes standing quietly there. "Holmes, thank goodness. Have the horsemen gone?"

"We were lucky, Watson. Milan is sure they were Bogachevich's henchmen from Cetinji."

"Do you suppose they are aware of our destination and have been following us?"

"Undoubtedly Dr. Krasich would have been forced to divulge our journey's end. Bogachevich is no fool. He would have tried to put himself in our shoes and inevitably would have speculated upon the route we would be taking."

"Then we are fortunate that they have missed us in the undergrowth, so to speak."

"Indeed, there is, however, one disadvantage we must now take into consideration. Our seekers are now between our destination and us and unless at some stage they double back upon themselves, will remain so. We have to ensure, therefore, that the distance between our two camps may be as broad as possible given our haste in the matter."

"Then we shall be following them!"

It was late on the next afternoon when at last we arrived above the town of Bejelo Polje. My first view of the town with its haze of smoking chimneys came as we rode down a cut in the craggy hillside and at last onto the main highway. To my great relief I also saw the station with a train in residence. Through the town gates we rode. I was relieved that upon this occasion our presence raised not a flicker of interest in the populace. Milan led us to a quiet row of oddly shaped and somewhat ramshackle buildings within yards of the station. He jumped down from his horse and called out.

"Alliah ... it is Spasich. Come out!"

For a few moments there was no sound, nor sight of any occupation. Then a door swung slowly open and an elderly man with a long unshaven face appeared.

The two men conversed in their own language for a short time with the elder considerably animated. Milan's brow began to darken. Then, quite forgetting our ignorance of the language, he cried out to us.

"Did you hear what he says? These swine of Bogachevich have been here this morning. They have attacked him and beaten him. Krasich has informed on us. He knows everything." Milan took the old man's arm and half dragged him into the declining afternoon light. "Look what one of them, Arakam has done to him."

Gently, I eased myself to the ground and took a closer look at the old man. His face was a mass of bruises.

"Good heavens," I cried. "Take the old man inside. Tell him I am a doctor and will do my best to assist him."

Milan helped Alliah back into his shack, little more than odd panels of wood and tarpaper. The roof was nothing more than sheets of rusty corrugated iron.

Fortunately I had retained in my pack the rudiments of my profession and gave the old man the best treatment I could.

He seemed pleased at my ministrations and thanked me profusely. Milan laughed. "Well done, Dr. Watson. Alliah thinks he will soon be as good as new."

"Is our friend able to tell us exactly what has happened?"

Milan took out his knife and ran his thumb-nail down the blade. He looked darkly at Holmes and myself. "Do not worry, when Arakan returns he will get much more than he bargains for."

Sherlock Holmes grasped Milan by the wrist and spoke in a sharp urgent tone. "No, Milan. Violence is not the answer, it will only induce further retaliation. The old man would not thank you for that."

Milan sighed.

"You are right, Mr. Holmes. Quick vengeance may bring slow revenge and we shall not be here to protect Alliah. Even so, it feels so unfair."

Once more we heard the sound of the train whistle. Holmes took out his watch and looked at it. "Six o'clock, we shall soon have to leave."

"Indeed," I said. "But we have yet to make provision for our journey to Belgrade. Our packs are quite empty and we have nothing to drink."

"I believe I can organise something, Dr. Watson," said Milan. "If Alliah can direct me to the nearest hostelry, I will obtain such provisions as we need."

The two Slavs conversed for a few moments. Then Milan disappeared into the growing twilight. As he took his leave, the cold evening air rushed into the shack. It occurred to me that the old man seemed to have very little in the way of heating in his home. I rubbed my hands together and pointed to the stoves and pulled a face, which in any language manifestly said 'I am cold'.

Holmes peered out of the tiny rear window into the yard beyond. "Ah, behold our fuel." He took the old man by the arm and pointed through the window. Then he too disappeared into the growing darkness only to re-appear a few moments later laden with broken planks of wood and logs; and so it was that a few minutes later there was a fire blazing in the stove and a warm glow filling the room.

Almost immediately Milan re-appeared. Over one shoulder he carried two bulging haversacks, over the other he carried a wine skin. Provisions enough (I sincerely hoped) for the journey.

Once more we donned our coats and hats and prepared to take our leave of Alliah. The old man was patently sad to see us go. He shook hands with each of us in turn. As we stepped out into the cold night air, I saw Holmes place some of the precious currency notes given to us by General Wilton, into Alliah's gnarled old hands.

As we turned into the station yard. I saw Holmes counting the money. "How much did you give the old man?" I asked.

"Something like four pounds," he admitted. "Although I believe it to be scant compensation for the service he has performed for us."

"Indeed," I agreed. "We can only hope that when Arakan returns he will not treat him too harshly."

"Amen to that, Watson," said Holmes with much feeling.

Quickly we boarded the train. The whistle gave three sharp blasts and we were on our way out of Montenegro and into Serbia and Belgrade, on the next leg of our journey to St. Petersburg.

Two

Our train rattled, squealed and bumped across the Serbian border and through the town of Prijepolje. The accommodation in which we found ourselves could in no way have been described as salubrious. The huge ancient engine was black with oil, grease and coal dust. The carriages, two in number, were situated between cattle trucks before and mineral trucks aft and were both dirty and smelly. The seats, however, no matter how old and tattered, were infinitely more comfortable and welcoming than the saddle I had inhabited for the last two days.

The matter of old Alliah, however, was continuing to exercise my mind. A mental picture of the angry return of Arakan was repeatedly forming in my head. Whilst I was explaining my concerns, however, Milan began to laugh. Somewhat surprised by his outburst, I remonstrated with the Serb. "I am sorry, Dr. Watson," he said. "But I was thinking of exactly the same thing."

"Indeed? Then perhaps you will explain how you have come to find the situation so amusing?"

Milan answered, "When I set out to search for supplies, I made directly to the house of Pasich; old Alliah had told me that it was the tavern used regularly by Bogachevich's men. It was then, that I saw the opportunity to have my revenge on Arakan for his treatment of the old man, and no harm done."

"I went to the stables and took the horses to Pasich's. The tavern is a large busy place, but I was fortunate enough to see him as I arrived. I told him 'Arakan has sent for these horses. Can you tell me where I can find him?' Pasich told me he was in the big room at the back. So I asked him to stable the horses for me while I found Arakan, because I needed permission to get supplies for my return journey to Montenegro.

"Pasich said that Arakan had insisted that he should not be disturbed, so if I told him what I needed, he would supply it and let Arakan know later. So I told him to be quick about it because Arakan wanted me to be quickly on my way.

"I expect that by then, Pasich was just as eager to be rid of me, as I was to leave, so he led me into the kitchen and told me to select what I needed and be on my way. So as you see from the pack you are looking into, Dr. Watson, there is best sausage, fruit, bread, cheese and onions, all taken at the expense of Arakan."

"You robber!" I cried. "I recall hearing the sound of horses after you left us, but it never occurred to me that it was you on your way to hoodwink our enemies."

I am not too sure how many stations there are between the Montenegro border and Belgrade. There may be twenty, I cannot remember. What I do recall, however, is the pedestrian pace of our train and the seemingly interminable time spent waiting at each of those out of the way halts.

Fortunately the night was somewhat less interrupted by these wearisome events and our party managed to sleep a little, but notwithstanding we arrived at the town of Carcak stiff and weary and longing for a soft bed with crisp sheets.

I rubbed my eyes and looked blearily at the rugged countryside as it moved slowly past our window.

The voice of Milan broke into my reverie. "It should not be too long before we enter Carcak," he said. "It is from there we take the train to Belgrade. I believe we have one hour and fifty minutes to wait."

"Excellent," said Holmes with enthusiasm.

"The time we have on our hands will provide us with an opportunity to discover if there is any news of our Russian friends."

"Indeed," I agreed. "It may also provide us with an opportunity to take a little breakfast."

Holmes chuckled. "Possibly, old fellow, possibly. Who knows, we may be fortunate enough to solve both external and internal questions."

The station proved to be both large and well built, but the town beyond, however, proved to be considerably less so and mainly consisted of wooden shacks lining dirt roads, with only a tiny number of stone built properties to break the monotony.

Despite the apparent poverty and faded air of the area in which we found ourselves, there was the usual hubbub I had come to associate with the region. Clearly the notion of being up with the lark had enormous currency hereabouts.

We quickly came to a town square with a deep river running along one side. Across the river, like a cat, its back arched in the face of an enemy lay an ancient stone bridge. Leaning over the wall and peering down into the river below was a young man, of perhaps twenty. He seemed to be the only person on view who was not actively engaged in some worthwhile enterprise. Milan shook hands with the young man and briefly conversed with him, asking him about the availability of a hot meal (I sincerely hoped!).

The young man shook his head. There was no establishment open at this hour. Then he brightened up. He had had as idea and we should follow him. On the way to our destination the two Serbs chatted happily, almost, it seemed to me, as if some bond existed between them. After the shortest journey we came through a high stone arch and into a building beyond.

"This is the house of Bosko Curcich, the father of our young friend, who is Bosko the younger. Bosko tells me that his mother will be pleased to provide us with a meal," said Milan.

The ready acceptance of three strangers and the willingness to assist and succour us, surprised me somewhat for a moment. Then I recalled the sign of the open palm shown to Bosko by Milan and the earlier encounter with the gatekeeper of Cetinji who had gone out of his way to co-operate with us. But Mrs. Curcich was at her door wearing a welcoming smile and such questions as I might ask needed to be postponed, but I resolved to discover the exact nature of this invisible bond at the earliest opportunity.

Before breakfasting, I had a wash, the first in three days. We breakfasted on eggs and bacon, another rare treat for my companions and myself, rarer, I discovered, for the general population of Carcak. Fortunately for us the Curich family were well-to-do and owned much of the land to the east of the town. Meat, Milan explained, was a rare indulgence, usually consumed on high days, holidays and at funeral wakes.

Of our Russian friends, the news was less satisfying, however. Bosko had heard nothing of any strangers, save ourselves, but as he quite rightly pointed out, they would not necessarily have revealed themselves. Even assuming they would have needed to do so, there were plenty of poor townsfolk, who, for a nominal sum, would have gladly aided them and promptly forgotten it, even if they had been suspicious of the motives of the Russians.

"But they surely could not witness a man being taken along against his will and simply stand by and do nothing?" I objected.

Milan had a ready answer, one, which I must confess, made me uncomfortable. "Leaving aside the possibility that your Mr. Andrews was drugged or presumed to be mad, Dr. Watson. What if those who co-operated with the Russians were simply so poor that the promise of hard cash encouraged them to be deaf, dumb and blind? Look around you, if you were living in such poverty, would your scruples not be thrown out of the window, so that tomorrow your family might eat?"

*****

A night and a day had almost passed as our train slowly carried us on the last lap of our journey to Belgrade. Milan promised us once there, we should have a bath, a bed and as much sleep as we could manage. The train had for some time run alongside the winding Jura river which ambled through a long valley bottom. We were travelling through what Milan called the valley of the seven towns. It was between the towns of Polenca and Sulianjac when the railway actually crossed the river; looking out of the window, we could see the line as it looped across the river, through the town and back again across the river once more.

As we approached the capital, the train contained less and less available space. Even though on this occasion there were no less than fives carriages, great numbers of people, from the lowest peasant to the highest official, were sitting or standing cheek by jowl. Fortunately, it was a corridor train so there was the possibility of some movement.

As we left the town of Polenca, Milan disappeared into the crowd in search of a pedlar who had come aboard selling sweet meats. Suddenly the train came to a shuddering halt and Holmes and I were almost thrown into each other. Disentangling himself from a large elderly lady and her equally large pack, Holmes struggled to the window trying to discover the reason for our sudden halt.

"Can you see what the cause of the obstruction is, Holmes?" I said.

"Indeed, there seems to be some kind of activity on the bridge ahead."

The train began to move slowly once more. Then with a great hiss of steam it came to another halt.

"There now seems to be a number of men on the bridge, some horsemen as well."

"What do you make of it, Holmes?" I cried.

But before Holmes could make his reply, Milan reappeared. Forcing his way through the crowd he grabbed me by the arm. "Bogachevich is here," he said breathlessly. "It is he who has stopped the train."

"Good heavens," I cried. "Are you certain?"

"Yes," he said flatly, "and Arakan has already boarded the train."

In stark contrast to the excitability of Milan and myself, Holmes was cool and calm. "There is no doubt that they are seeking us. We have heaped too many humiliations upon them to just let us go." He gazed keenly at Milan and myself. "I do not have to impress upon you the seriousness of the situation in which we find ourselves. Milan, where did you observe Arakan?"

"It was in the first carriage, I had just found the pedlar when the train suddenly stopped. The door burst open and there he was with Bogachevich at the trackside urging him on."

Holmes picked up the haversacks and threw one at me. "We must make our way to the rear of the train, quickly now!"

Milan ducked out into the corridor, he suppressed a cry of alarm. "It is Arakan, he has just entered the carriage."

Holmes thrust the wineskin into the hands of the dismayed Serb. "Here, if necessary use this as a weapon."

Through the congested corridors we pushed our way until at last we reached the rear of the train. We found ourselves in a guard's van which although stacked with crates of produce, was fortunately devoid of human occupation. Holmes pulled at a lever and a sliding door opened slowly on creaking runners. Looking quickly out into the cool, late afternoon air, he smiled and made a little noise of satisfaction. "Excellent, the coast is clear, come Watson. This is where we disembark."

Milan took one quick look outside and jumped nimbly down to the track. Holmes sat on the edge and swung his legs out. He eased himself over the side and disappeared. Immediately his head and shoulders appeared once more. "Hurry, Watson. Throw down the haversacks, we have little time to spare."

I did as I was told and with the help of Milan found myself on the track side, and whilst I collected up the haversacks, Holmes and Milan slid the door closed again. For a brief moment we stood there. I quickly looked around. There was no hiding place and at any moment we might be discovered. Then Holmes grabbed me by the arm. "Quickly, Watson, under the train."

Throwing the haversacks before me, I scrambled between the wheels and lay face down on the track bed. Milan spared no time in following me, but Holmes waited just long enough to throw a few personal items from his pocket towards the embankment. His golden signet ring I noticed with some dismay was among these items. It landed squarely atop the banking and lay glittering in the glow of the slanting sun.

A number of riders came clattering along the track side, followed by several running men. There was much shouting of orders and of angry replies. Clearly our pursuers were becoming frustrated at their inability to find us.

Then I heard a voice, one I clearly recognised. It was Bogachevich. He was very angry and shouting curses (Milan later informed me) at his men. Then, one of them happened upon the items Holmes had thrown. He shouted to Bogachevich, who moved at last into sight.

A short burst of conversation followed. Two of the men were sent up the embankment to investigate further. Then one stumbled upon the ring. He gave a loud cry and held it up for inspection.

Milan and I were lying with our heads almost touching. "What are they saying?" I whispered into his ear.

"The man has told Bogachevich that he has found the foreigner's ring." He listened intently for a moment. "Bogachevich is telling him that the scum, that is us, have escaped the train and must be making back for Polenca. But one of us has been careless, so the trail must lead that way."

The train whistle suddenly sounded and the engine burst into life once more. The brakes squealed and the train inched forward. The men began to run back along the track and the riders spurred on their horses and quickly disappeared in the direction of the town.

Hoping that there was no one left to observe us, I ducked between the slowly turning wheels and back onto the trackside. Holmes and Milan swiftly followed. As the train moved so did we. Keeping low and as close to the carriages as possible, we moved closer and closer to the bridge.

"We are only a few yards from the bridge," said Holmes in my ear. "We must hide under it."

A great iron support loomed up before me. I threw my haversack down the banking and followed it without thought. My only concern was to hide myself from terrible danger. Slipping and sliding, I found myself disappearing into the darkness before coming out into dappled light by the waterside where a large wooden platform met the water. Swiftly I was joined by Holmes and Milan, whilst above us the train now picked up speed and roared and rattled over the bridge and away to Belgrade.

For quite some time we sat huddled together on the wooden pontoon, hardly daring to speak above a whisper. Because of our fear of discovery we waited for dusk to fall before deciding to move on.

Sherlock Holmes held his watch up to the fading rays of sunlight, which came through the iron footway above his head. "Five o'clock," he murmured. "It will soon be dark."

"We cannot stay here all night," said Milan. "At this time of the year it still gets too cold to remain out in the open."

"Indeed," Holmes agreed. "I believe, however, that I can see just a little way along the river the sanctuary we need."

Standing up I followed the line of his outstretched finger along the river bank to a small hut almost surrounded by trees.

"Hmm. It does not look particularly salubrious."

"Salubrious or not, Watson," said Holmes firmly. "We have no choice but to try our luck there. The hut's facilities may be somewhat Spartan, but I have no doubt that it will be infinitely preferable to a night in the open."

One by one we crawled from our hiding place and into the open. A cold wind was blowing across the valley and rippling the surface of the river. There was the smell of rain in the air. The riverbank was presently completely deserted, but for how long this favourable situation would hold we could not tell, so we quickly moved along the footpath to the temporary safety of the little waterside hut.

Quite as expected, it quickly came on to rain. The wooded area afforded a little shelter, but as the downpour intensified, there was no hiding place save for the hut. Sherlock Holmes peered through the tiny window, but in the growing darkness was unable to perceive much of the interior.

"There is no light," he said. Stepping back a pace he looked up at the chimney. "And no smoke. It would seem that there is nobody at home."

Milan tried the door. It was securely locked, but this was not a situation which lasted for very long, however. He produced his knife and quickly proceeded to spring the lock. He laughed "It is a simple mechanism, easily forced."

I recalled the little pouch of brass instruments Holmes habitually carried and had so successfully employed in Italy when entering the Bixio Clinic to rescue Mycroft, his brother. "It would seem that you have a little competition, Holmes."

His reply was sharp and incisive. "I believe, Doctor, that we should derive greater utility from a discussion on the housebreaking prowess of Milan from the inside of the property than we should from standing out here in the porchway, with the rain dripping down our necks."

Milan pushed open the door and peered inside the hut. He beckoned for us to follow. Holmes produced his Vesta case and struck one of the matches. The flare of yellow light briefly lit up the hut's interior. To my surprise, I saw it was remarkably tidy and well kept. Espying an adjacent candle, I lit it from Holmes's match. The soft golden light threw up giant shadows on the walls and furnishings. There was a table and three chairs, a camp bed with several blankets piled neatly upon it, a number of large and small cupboards lining the walls and at the farthest end of the room there stood a large cast-iron wood burner.

"This is indeed a little home from home," I remarked. "My word, old Alliah would regard this as luxury accommodation and no mistake."

"Clearly this is no casual stopping off place or repository," said Holmes. "Someone has regular usage of this hut and it is quite possible that the owner may return at any time. We shall have to be on our guard."

I gazed longingly at the bed. "I suppose that means we must keep watch all night?"

Holmes chuckled. No doubt he had read my thoughts. "I am sorry, old fellow. That is exactly what it means. But never mind, we will light a fire and take something hot; then we shall all feel better," he smiled his tight little smile. "And Watson, if you feel a desire to sleep, then why not? We can take the night in shifts and still manage a little slumber."

Much cheered up at the prospect of sleep, my mind turned to the matter of the fire. "Dare we take the risk? Someone may notice the smoke and come to investigate. The immediate hue and cry for us may have died down, but I have no doubt that there will still be many unfriendly eyes watching out for any sign of us."

Holmes frowned, "I really believe that we have little choice. It is only early evening and the air is even now very cold. To pass the night without heat would be particularly uncomfortable."

"Our discovery would also be particularly uncomfortable," I reminded him.

"Then we shall have to rely on our own vigilance and the supposition of others that we are the legal inhabitants of this hut."

The matter settled, we prepared to light a fire. Beside the stove, Holmes discovered a bundle of old newspapers and some kindling. Milan remembered he had earlier noticed a pile of logs in the porch and he quickly collected an armful.

"We shall keep the damper fully open," said Holmes. "Perhaps it will minimise the smoke from the chimney."

Cold and tired as I was, thirst was also my enemy. Looking into the depths of my haversack I extracted the three horn cups given to me at the start of our journey from Cetinji by Dr. Krasich. Fortunately they had remained undamaged despite the rough handling of my pack. Milan's wineskin had also emerged unscathed from its journey and I was able to pour three good measures of wine into the cups. Taking the poker from the fire I plunged it into the cups and there emerged a hissing and bubbling and the warm smell of mulled wine. I handed the drinks around and held my own up in a salute. "Good health, gentlemen. Here's to a quiet night."

*****

It was as if only the briefest of moments had elapsed before I was brought sharply back into the waking world.

"Watson, my dear fellow, wake up," It was Holmes shaking me gently.

"Holmes, what is it? What is happening?"

"It appears that the owner of the hut is returning."

Forgetting all notions of sleep I jumped to my feet and joined Milan who was peering out of the riverside window. A long narrow boat with a tall white sail had pulled in alongside the hut. A light shone brightly from the mast and this allowed us an excellent view of the boat and its single occupant. He was a tall thin man, with dark hair and a large drooping moustache. As a protection against the elements, he wore a huge black oilskin.

"What are we to do?" I asked Holmes. "If this fellow is the rightful tenant, he will hardly be delighted to discover his property to be full of uninvited occupants."

Milan chuckled. "There are three of us to his one. It will hardly matter if he is pleased or not."

"But we should be fair to him," I objected. "It is not his fault that we have taken up illegal possession. We should not be violent with him."

"Then what do you suggest, Dr. Watson? That we should send out an emissary to warn him of our presence?"

"And why not?" said Holmes. "Our man deserves the opportunity to give us a friendly welcome." He held up a lamp, which he obviously must have discovered whilst I was sleeping. "Here, Milan. Take this and go out, call to him. Tell him we are travellers, who have lost our way and have sought succour at his door. Say that we have done his property no damage and mean him no harm. Ask him if he will accept our hand of friendship?"

Milan looked dubiously at Holmes for a moment, but he took up the lamp nevertheless.

"Very well, Mr. Holmes. I will do what I can."

Sherlock Holmes and I watched through the riverside window as Milan made his approach to the boat. The tall man gave quite a start as he heard the voice of our emissary. For a few moment they conversed, Milan gesturing towards the hut on several occasions. Then he and the boat owner laughed and shook hands. I looked at Holmes.

"Evidently they have come to an understanding," I said.

The door opened and the boatman entered. He removed his oilskins and hung them on a peg behind the door and stood for a moment surveying us. "You are Holmes and Watson?" he said in a thick voice. "Your names are well broadcast in these parts. Some are keen to have you dead."

A shiver ran down my spine, it was discomforting to know that our lives were in such danger.

"But do not worry, I am not one of those people."

Sherlock Holmes held out his hand. "I am Holmes, this is Dr. Watson. Milan you know. I am glad to discover, sir, that you are not supportive of our enemies. But you have the advantage of us. You are our provider, our confessor and our protector, yet we do not know your name."

The boatman took Holmes's hand and shook it warmly. "I am Zoltan Szibor, but please call me just Zoltan."

"You are not Serbian?"

"I am Hungarian, but my allegiance is to myself. I am just as much an enemy of that despot Franz Josef as the Serbs, or indeed the Bosnians," he picked up his pack and dumped it upon the table. "I am an enemy of all dictators and warlords and that is why you are safe from Bogachevich as long as you are with me."

The Hungarian sat down at the table and began to empty his pack. "The word on the river is that you are fugitives from the wrath of Bogachevich because you have stolen valuables belonging to him; and that he has issued a reward for your capture, dead if necessary," said Zoltan evenly.

"You are not interested in a reward?" said Holmes.

"Bogachevich has not enough money to buy my loyalty. He is a crook who dresses himself up as an honest politician. I do not want his blood money."

Zoltan surveyed the produce of his trip. "Is anyone hungry?"

It was only a short time later when, satisfied at the table, we sat around the stove smoking a long-awaited pipe. Holmes had said very little during the meal. At one point I had watched him and had observed that he was formulating something in his mind.

Zoltan looked at his watch. "It is already past one a.m.," he said. "If I am to make you gentlemen comfortable for the night, then I need to go back to my boat and collect the straw mattresses I have stored there. Will someone help me?"

Milan rose from his seat and rubbed his hands together.

"Lead on, sir. I will carry your boat upon my back if it means a good night's sleep."

A little later, a warm and snug household was bedded down for the night. The accommodation was rather cramped and the sleeping facilities consisted of little more than straw-filled palliasses and a coarse blanket, but all the riches of Croesus would not have bought us a safer bed and a more friendly house.

*****

It was morning when next I opened my eyes. The air was filled with the aroma of coffee. Only Milan seemed to be visible. "Good morning, Dr. Watson. Will you have some coffee?"

The door opened and Holmes and Zoltan appeared. Over his shoulder, Holmes was carrying a large, coarsely woven bag. "Ah, coffee," he said. "And here is breakfast." He deposited the bag onto the table.

"What on Earth have you got there?" I queried.

"Four large river trout."

Whilst Zoltan prepared the fish he raised the subject of our journey. Briefly, Holmes explained our mission. He also admitted to the uncertainty of our immediate future.

"We had planned to travel to Belgrade, then take another train to the Roumanian border," Holmes sighed. "Unfortunately, we are now caught on the horns of a dilemma. At best we are two days behind our quarry, but are unable to take the quickest route because of the situation in which we find ourselves," he looked at Zoltan. "I believe, therefore, we must adopt a reserve plan of action."

Holmes took his map of the region from his jacket pocket and spread it out on the table. "Here, Watson, is the way we have come, and here is Polenca and here is the Jura River. We are roughly here. Now, the train was taking us to Belgrade and there is no other for two days and even if we desire to take the next train, we will be unable so to do. We cannot go to town, neither can we walk to the next town, as without doubt all roads will be watched. I do not believe we can even go back the way we have come, at least for several days. As for staying here, I cannot see how we can, for as surely as night follows day, Bogachevich's men must eventually investigate here as well."

"Then what is your proposal, Holmes?"

"That Zoltan shall take us to Belgrade on his boat."

The Hungarian nodded his assent. "Mr. Holmes and I discussed the matter when we were catching our breakfast, and speaking of which," he said smiling, "I believe that the fish is now quite ready. So please come to the table, gentlemen."

Breakfast over and the inner man fortified, we prepared for our river journey. Holmes insisted on us removing every trace of our existence in the hut, such was his concern for the future safety of our guardian. "If the forces of Bogachevich discover that Zoltan has not only harboured us, but has also engineered our escape, they will not treat him kindly. We need only to recall how old Alliah was maltreated, merely upon suspicion of co-operating with us."

Very soon the boat was made ready for our expedition. Zoltan calculated that the journey would take just under ten hours, a slow route, but one that promised to be infinitely safer than any other quicker alternative.

The daylight showed Zoltan's boat to be over thirty feet long. Below there was a somewhat cramped cabin, only just large enough for us all. But beyond there was a capacious storage area, in which Zoltan cheerfully admitted to us that, during the years of conflict between the Slavs and the Turks, he had once carried a dozen heavily armed men, complete with barrels of blasting powder, from Belgrade to Leskovach, a town near the Albanian border where they had taken part in an armed insurrection.

Then from above there came a cry. It was the voice of Milan. His face, flushed with excitement, appeared in the hatchway. "Mr. Holmes, riders are approaching from the direction of the town."

"Stay here," said Zoltan. "I will see. Milan, did they observe you?"

"No, I do not think so."

"Then get below with the others, possibly they may be making general enquiries." He stopped at the top of the steps and looked calmly down upon us. "I will tell them that I came back late last night and know nothing of their mission."

Zoltan disappeared on deck and as he closed the hatch we were enveloped in darkness. We could clearly hear the sound of the horse's hooves as the riders drew nearer. Then, as they came alongside, there was a shout from one of the riders. Milan, who had followed Zoltan up the steps, opened the hatch very slightly. Cautiously, he peered out.

"Can you see anything?" I asked him.

He shook his head. "Nothing, but I dare not open the hatch anymore for fear of being noticed. I will just have to listen to their conversation."

"What are they saying?" said Holmes.

"The rider is asking Zoltan if he has seen any strangers. Zoltan is telling him he has seen nothing and is asking why they want to know. Now the rider is telling him that they are seeking three thieves, two foreigners and a renegade Serb."

The conversation above us continued. Holmes again asked for a translation.

"The riders have been instructed to search all houses and outbuildings for signs of us. Zoltan is telling them that he is inviting them to do so."

Milan gave a sharp intake of breath.

"What is wrong?" I asked.

"They are insisting on searching the boat. Zoltan is trying to dissuade them, but they are insisting." Milan grimaced, "I think we may be in trouble."

Quickly, I looked around our accommodation. There was no hiding place. Clearly if we could not hide, then we would fight. I looked across at Holmes. He had his pistol in his hand.

"Watson," he said urgently. "There is a small area behind the steps into which I intend to secrete myself. When the riders come below, Milan and yourself must act as if your are resigned to captivity. You must attract all their attention so I may act unobserved." He quickly squeezed his lean frame into the cramped space. "Here they come, gentlemen. Let us see how we may handle them."

Milan hardly had enough time to join me at the foot of the steps, before the hatch opened and the cabin was flooded with light. Zoltan appeared at the top of the steps. Behind him a large bearded man loomed. He gave the Hungarian a violent push which sent him tumbling down into the cabin below and into a heap at our feet. The bearded man shouted over his shoulder to his companions. Milan whispered into my ear. "It is Arakan, he is telling two of his men, Radovan and Radko, to ride back to town and fetch the Wolf. He is telling another, Dragan, to watch the top of the boat."

The Serb came cautiously down the steps, in his hand he held a large glistening knife. He eyed us suspiciously. "You are the foreign swine?"

"We are Watson and Spasich," I said.

"The Englishman and the renegade," he growled. "So where is the other Englishman?"

Milan and I looked at each other in mock astonishment.

"I do not understand. To whom are you referring?" I asked innocently.

Zoltan had regained his wits and began to rise from the floor, but Arakan placed the sole of his boot into his back and forced him none-too gently once more into a prone position. "You, boatman. Where are you hiding the foreigner?"

"You will never find him," I said sharply.

Arakan stamped on Zoltan's back. The boatman gave a little cry of pain as the Serb ground the heel of his boot into the Hungarian's spine. Once more, I had to control Milan's outburst of temper as he rose angrily from his seat to confront the bandit. On this occasion, however, my intervention did me little service. Arakan's hand came quickly towards me and before I knew it, the blade of his knife was pressed firmly against my throat. "Do you take me for a idiot, Englishman? I am Arakan. Your play acting will not fool me." He glared at me, his bearded face inches from mine. Do not lie to me. You know where he is. Now you will tell me!"

At this he threw me back against the cabin wall. My head struck something hard and I saw stars. Then before I could collect my scattered senses, Sherlock Holmes struck. He was across the cabin before I knew it. The butt of his pistol came crashing down on Arakan's unsuspecting head. The Serb staggered forward then fell senseless into the waiting arms of Milan.

"Good work, Mr. Holmes," he said.

"Watson, are you hurt?" Holmes anxiously asked me.

"No, my dear fellow, a slight knock only."

Milan knelt by the prostrate Zoltan. "Are you in much pain, my friend?" he asked the boatman.

Zoltan groaned. "Not too much, my friend." Gingerly he rose to his feet and carefully felt his back. Gazing at the unconcious bandit, he smiled. "But not as hurt as friend Arakan, I think."

Sherlock Holmes took Milan by the arm. "If we are to make a successful escape, we must act quickly. Call out to Dragan. Tell him to join us down below."

Milan did as he was bid, and immediately the face of a young brown-haired man appeared in the open hatchway. It is quite possible, that in his life he was the recipient of many surprises, both pleasurable and unpleasant, but it is doubtful whether the young Serb was ever more surprised, pleasantly or otherwise; for without demur or warning, the long arm of Sherlock Holmes was around his neck and he was pitched headlong into the cabin.

"Now," said Holmes calmly as he surveyed the prostrate forms before us. "Zoltan, you must prepare to cast off as quickly as possible. Milan and I will secure these villains until we come across a favourable site on which we may safely deposit them." He took a length of coarse twine from the large bale in the corner of the cabin and, with Arakan's knife, he cut it into several convenient lengths. "Now, we have them quickly rendered harmless."

Coming from above I, could hear the chug of the engine and the rattle and clatter as Zoltan fed the furnace. Holmes and Milan dragged the senseless Serbs into the hold, whilst I attempted to tidy away some of the wreckage of our most unpleasant encounter.

Sherlock Holmes took out his watch and scanned it with a worried eye.

"The horsemen will have by now reached the town. All we may hope for is the possibility that they will not immediately locate Bogachevich and that we shall have the opportunity to escape."

"Indeed," I agreed. "Perhaps I should go on deck and see what I can do to assist Zoltan?"

I had scarcely reached the top of the stairs when the Hungarian called out to me. "Dr. Watson, I have a full head of steam now. Will you cast off?"

The boat slipped forward into the middle of the river. Zoltan looked at me, and smiled. "So far, so good. But we are not quite out of the woods. The river ahead is very straight for the next five kilometres and any pursuer will undoubtedly see us."

I turned to Zoltan. "Is there any place along the river where we may seek refuge?"

Zoltan shook his head. "It is many kilometres before we reach such a place, Dr. Watson."

The heads of Sherlock Holmes and Milan appeared in the hatchway. Holmes was disappointed with our situation. He smacked his right fist into his left hand. "If we had only departed under the cover of darkness. This is all my fault, Watson; *mea culpa*."

"Nonsense, Holmes," I cried. "Last evening we were quite exhausted and simply unable to travel any further. You cannot blame yourself."

Suddenly Milan pointed over my shoulder. "Look," he cried. "Riders."

The riders were swiftly overtaking us, eight men dressed in sheepskin jerkins riding pell-mell along the towpath. As they drew level with the boat the leader reached for his belt and pulled out a long black pistol.

I saw a flash from the muzzle of the gun, followed by a loud bang. I threw myself onto the deck and felt in my pocket for my service revolver. There was little cover on the boat and I felt dreadfully exposed.

A shout came from the riverbank.

"He is telling us to stop," said Milan. "Or they will shoot us like dogs."

I gritted my teeth and did my utmost to quell the sharp wave of anger I felt rising in my breast. Retaliation, I realised, was not the answer. We were too exposed and any of our party might be shot, perhaps fatally. No, any solution would be brought about by a cool head and a calm reaction.

Holmes, his eyes flashing, took Zoltan by the arm. "Do as you are bid," he said. "But be very careful to keep to the bank farthest from our enemies." He looked at Milan. "Keep them talking. Say to them that we are experiencing problems with our steering, I need a little time to think."

Milan looked doubtfully at Holmes for a moment, but he nodded his assent.

"Holmes," I said eagerly. "You have an idea?"

He looked thoughtfully at me. "Quite so, Doctor. Look at the riverbank on the side of the riders. She how marshy it is becoming. How far do you suppose they will be able to ride before their horses become hopelessly bogged down in the mire?"

I quickly followed his line of sight. "Hmm ... yes. I see what you mean, Holmes. I should judge that it would not be too far ... but look, there is a wooden bridge. They will simply ride their horses across it and onto the dry bank."

"The bridge," said Holmes, smiling his tight little smile. "What do you make of the bridge?"

"It is an old wooden structure but not sufficiently weak to collapse when a number of riders take their horses across it."

Holmes laughed and shook his head. "No, my dear fellow. I do not hope for the collapse of the bridge under the weight of horse. I do, however, hope that it may be pulled to its destruction."

"Excellent," I said. "I wonder, however, if our enemies are simply going to sit quietly by and watch us as we carry out our plan of action."

"No, indeed," Holmes agreed. "So this is where we invoke the assistance of our friend Arakan." He turned to Milan. "Tell our pursuers that we are holding their esteemed leader our prisoner."

Milan did as he as bid. A ripple of urgent talk spread amongst our pursuers. Then the leading rider shouted back his reply.

"He is asking to see Arakan, because he doesn't believe us."

"Very well," said Holmes. "Tell them that we will bring Arakan on deck to prove we are no liars." He signalled to Zoltan that the bandit should be brought up for inspection.

A few moments later Zoltan re-appeared with the bound and still somewhat stunned Arakan. Even from such a distance a sharp intake of breath could be heard from the river bank. Holmes grasped the Serb by the collar. "Tell them that they must stop pursuing us, Arakan," said Holmes. "Tell them that if they agree to return to Polenca we shall release Dragan and yourself somewhere upon the river bank for later collection. But if they continue to follow us we shall throw you into the river where you will most assuredly drown."

In a hoarse voice, Arakan shouted Holmes's instructions. From the riverbank there came a chorus of cries and oaths, but the horsemen began to obey, slowly they turned their horses around and trotted them off towards the town.

"Very good," said Holmes evenly. "Zoltan, do you have some rope on board?"

I smiled at the mystified boatman. "We are going to pull the bridge down."

For a moment he stood there with a look of blank amazement on his face, then he threw back his head and laughed loudly. "Ha! Mr. Holmes, you are a genius."

The boat had continued to drift slowly towards the bridge. Zoltan steered us as close to the bank as safety would allow. Then, like a cat, the Hungarian jumped onto the riverbank. Holmes lashed one end of the rope to a convenient bulwark, then he coiled it up and threw it into the waiting hands of the boatman. Immediately Zoltan ran along the riverbank to the bridge and tied the rope to one of its ancient and rickety supports.

Arakan, suddenly realising the meaning of our actions, struggled free from Milan's grip and shouted at the top of his voice. He was swiftly seized again but not before the riders had stopped in their tracks.

"He has warned them about our intentions," Milan cried.

"The riders are returning," said Holmes. "Hurry, Zoltan."

Quickly the Hungarian ran back along the bank and jumped back on board. He threw forward a lever in the wheelhouse. The engine roared into life once more and we began to move quickly under the bridge.

The sound of gunfire came from the direction of the far bank. The riders had unleashed a volley of shots. A bullet sang past my head. I drew my revolver and looked across to Holmes. He also had his gun in his hand. Taking what cover the wheelhouse allowed, Holmes fired three times at our pursers and I, once.

I looked over the side of the boat to see how much rope there was left to run. Suddenly it sprang clear of the water dripping and covered in weed.

"Holmes," I cried. "We are about to discover whether your plan is a success."

A sudden jerk made me stagger slightly, the boat seemed to momentarily stand still, then with another jerk we jumped forward again. From behind us there came the crackling and grinding of a bridge falling to its doom, swiftly followed by cries of anger and dismay from the bank. Holmes had gambled, but he had gambled well. The old bridge was too weak to withstand our attack upon its ancient and venerable timbers. It swayed and buckled, then with a huge splash fell into the cold waters of the Jura River.

For a few moments both parties stood in awed silence. Then there erupted a great roar, ours a cheer of triumph, theirs a cry of despair and rage.

Sherlock Holmes and I shook hands.

"My dear fellow," I cried. "Congratulations."

"Thank you, Watson. *Carpe diem*, I believe."

*****

Our journey now became somewhat less fraught, we had left the minions of Bogachevich far behind us and as a consequence our hearts felt considerably lighter. Arakan and Dragan, we deposited a mile or so before the boat entered the Five Fingers. They were securely bound to each other, and as we pulled away, Holmes took Arakan's knife and hurled it as far as he was able along the riverbank. It landed some thirty feet away from the Slavs.

"There they go," he chuckled, as he watched Arakan and Dragan scrambling and tumbling after the knife. "When they finally extricate themselves, they will have no idea which of the forks in the river we have taken."

Milan was for cutting their throats, but Holmes and I refused point-blank. He looked calmly at the Serb and shook his head.

Milan was clearly unconvinced. As he turned away and disappeared down the steps into the cabin below, I could hear him mutter, "Dead men tell no tales."

The day began to grow both warm and sunny. Spring, it seemed had finally arrived. Only Sherlock Holmes and myself were on deck. Milan and Zoltan had retired to the hold and were rummaging around for some bottles of wine. The boat chugged steadily along whilst Holmes and I sat either side of the tiller in our shirtsleeves.

"Holmes?"

"Yes, my dear fellow?"

"The future of Zoltan is concerning me somewhat."

Holmes nodded. "I am afraid that you are exactly right, Watson. Zoltan will be *persona non grata* in these parts for as long as Bogachevich reigns." Holmes looked at me with serious eyes. "It is also my fear that his life will, likewise, not be worth a penny piece."

"The same consideration has unfortunately occurred to me, Mr. Holmes." It was Zoltan. His head and shoulders were just visible above the hatchway. He held a bottle of wine in each hand and he was smiling, clearly the prospect of an uncertain future seemed to worry him very little.

Zoltan placed the bottles onto the deck and came and sat on the locker from which we had earlier extracted the rope. "I shall be quite honest, gentlemen. For some time it has been my intention to return to my home and family. In another year or two, when I had saved enough money to keep me in comfort for the rest of my days, I meant to sail my boat back to Budapest, where I would hole up in some backwater," he sighed. "But now it seems I shall have to return home earlier than expected. It is a pity, but there it is." Zoltan stood up again. He smiled. "Forgive me my disappointments, gentlemen. I know that my worries are trivial when compared to the matters which are forcing you across this region. I am just a day or two from my home, whilst you are set to travel even further into the unknown." Zoltan picked up the bottles and returned to the hatch. He turned and looked at us, his eyes bright once more. "Now let us forget our worries for a while. A drink, we shall have a drink."

After luncheon, which had been taken on deck in the warm sunshine, Milan broached the subject of our possible reception in Belgrade.

"It seems to me that Bogachevich will have his spies out and as soon as we reach Belgrade there will be a welcoming committee waiting for us."

I looked at Holmes. There was considerable trepidation in my heart. Milan, of course, was exactly right. We could expect no soft beds with crisp sheets, only a prison cell awaiting us.

"Milan is correct, but what are we to do?" Holmes pulled a face and sighed.

"I believe that we have only one option open to us, Watson. If Zoltan is agreeable we shall take the river journey to Roumania." Holmes reached into his jacket pocket and took out the map. He spread it out on the roof of the wheelhouse and pointed to our present position. "Here is the Jura. Just before it reaches Belgrade, it forks. The left-hand fork runs into the heart of the city … there. The right hand fork, however, bypasses the city and heads off into the direction of the Danube … there. The Danube forms the border between Serbia and Roumania and it will take us where we need to go. This, Watson, is the route we must now take."

*****

The journey between the outskirts of Belgrade and the joining of the rivers Jura and Danube was thankfully uneventful. As the boat chugged its slow and steady way, like the walrus and the carpenter, we talked of many things. There was considerable discussion about our mission and the very real fears Holmes and I felt for the fate of Hunter Andrews, and the very real possibility that despite our best efforts our enemies would still thwart us.

Zoltan frowned and chewed his lip reflectively. "It may interest you, Mr. Holmes, that before my return to Polenca, I heard a most interesting conversation between some Russian workers in a Belgrade café. At the time, it meant nothing to me, but now upon reflection, it is as you say, the shilling has fallen."

Holmes laughed. "I think, Zoltan, you will find it is the penny has dropped."

"Exactly," said Zoltan. Shilling or penny, let me tell you what I heard. I had gone down to the Café Magya, just off one of Belgrade's main thoroughfares. In the past, I have done much trade there and I know many of the patrons. On this occasion my friend was busy with another trader, so I sat at a vacant table and waited for him to join me there. Then into the café came a party of men. By their accents I knew them to be Russians. For a while they talked in their own language, then another man joined them. He was a Croat trader so they all turned to talking in Serbo-Croat.

"After a good deal of arguing about a quantity of merchandise the Russians had to sell, they ordered vodka to seal the transaction. After several glasses they became more relaxed and engaged in idle conversation with the trader. One of the Russians asked him if he had seen the madman running through the streets by the river."

Holmes and I looked at each other as Zoltan continued his narration. "The trader shook his head and declared he had heard nothing because he had only arrived in Belgrade that morning, so the Russian said that sometime towards the noon hour the day before, four men had arrived at the station on the Montenegro train. One of these travellers seemed to be acting most oddly. It had been supposed that they were either Montenegrins or Serbs. Then, as they approached the main concourse, the odd one seemed to break free from his companions and began shouting and screaming in a language no one recognised or understood. His companions seemed quite taken aback and he was able to escape them. The interesting thing was Mr. Holmes, the man looked as if he might be a native of the area. He was black-haired and had a swarthy skin, indeed he looked very like the gypsies of the region."

"Hunter Andrews!" I cried.

"The very same," said Holmes, firmly.

"What happened to the man?" I asked.

"The fellow who was telling the story said that he approached the newcomers and asked if he might be of any assistance. They answered him in Russian and told him that their companion was a harmless mental incompetent, who was being taken to an asylum in St. Petersburg for treatment. Even so he could not be allowed to remain at large because he might be a danger to himself, so would he and his friends aid them in their search for him?"

"What happened, Zoltan?" Holmes asked the Hungarian, unable to keep the concern out of his voice.

"Well, apparently they spent most of that afternoon searching for the fellow. In the end he was cornered near the city walls. I suppose being hampered by the language barrier, he was always going to be caught. Now, from what you have told me, Mr. Holmes, it is quite clear to me that the madman was without question your Mr. Andrews."

*****

The night had almost passed. We had slept fitfully in the cramped accommodation the boat offered. We had travelled almost to the point where Holmes and myself would be going in one direction and our friends would be departing in the another; when goodbyes would have to be said.

A dark and heavy mist overhung the Danube, a wide and majestic highway which, if we wished, would take us to the Black Sea and warmer climes. Our destination, however, led us to the East then to the North with its unknown dangers.

We pulled in at a quiet landing stage on the Roumanian side of the river. Before us lay the magnificent Iron Gate, a deep cut gorge in the high banks, presently shrouded from our gaze, a sight, Zoltan informed us, equal to any in the whole of the Balkans.

He pointed to a pathway, which wandered away into the darkness, and although stiff and difficult, it led us to the nearest town.

We sat on boxes piled on the landing stage and in the glow of Zoltan's cabin lamp we made our farewells. Holmes held his hand out to Milan. "My dear fellow," he said. "We owe you an immense debt of gratitude. I hope we shall meet again one day."

"Thank you, Mr. Holmes," said the Serb taking his hand. "I do not know if your wish will be granted. Before me, I have a task which will place me in as much danger as I can handle." He laughed. "I have friends who will in all probability get me killed one day. But whatever my fate, sir, remember me kindly."

For myself, words so much a part of my life, both written and oral, failed me completely. It was with a moist eye, I shook the hand of one of the bravest men it has been my good fortune to call 'friend'.

"Goodbye, dear Doctor," he said, hugging me warmly. "When you return to London, look out for Spasich and the Black Hand in your newspapers ... Goodbye." Then he was gone, back to the refuge of the boat's cabin.

Zoltan reached up to the boat deck and took down our two haversacks. Again they were full almost to bursting point. An earlier stop at Kurach, on the Serbian side of the river had allowed us to spend our remaining money on supplies for Holmes and myself and a quantity of wood and coal for the boat. Zoltan was well known at the trading post and experienced no difficulty with the transaction. We did, however, hear the interesting tale about a rascally band of foreigners who had held up and robbed a prominent local politician from Montenegro. Descriptions of these desperados were vague, but it was thought that they might be Chinese!

Zoltan held up his watch to the lamp and smiled. "It is almost five-thirty. Soon it will be light. If you keep to the path above the landing stage, you will have no problems. Do not forget that many Roumanians speak French and if you remember your schoolboy Latin, you may even be able to converse in Pidgin-Roumanian. Good luck to you both."

With a parting wave, the Hungarian scrambled aboard his boat. Then the engine roared into life once more, and with the bow-wave turning into white horses behind her, the boat chugged into the middle of the river and disappeared slowly into the mist.

Sherlock Holmes stood up and pulled on a haversack. Picking up the other, he held it out to me.

"Come along, my dear fellow," he said briskly. "Roumania awaits us."

Three

Although the path was steep in places, it proved to be safe and well constructed. At last the early spring sunshine broke through and flooded the countryside in its bright warm embrace. Now we could see the Iron Gate in all its natural beauty. The wild spring flowers, the craggy outcrops and the twisted trees in new leaf all waking up to the new season.

When at last we reached the top of the path, Holmes and I sat for a short while catching our breath. Yet, despite the stiff climb, I felt invigorated and ready to face whatever fate should throw at me.

After our short break we pushed on quickly leaving the Iron Gate behind us. Soon we came to a road. A sharp breeze was blowing little dust devils as we turned our faces to the South. Then, from behind us came a rumbling noise. Clearly we were being overtaken by a heavy vehicle. Being strangers in a strange land, Holmes and I decided that discretion should be the better part of valour, so we waited in a small copse by the roadside until the exact nature of the vehicle and the demeanour of its passengers could be ascertained.

Then, from around the corner a large steam driven leviathan appeared. At the helm stood a tall, raw-boned young man. We stepped back into the road and Holmes hailed the driver in French. "Good day to you, sir. We are needing to get to Orsova. Are you able to take us at least part of the way?"

The young man pulled a lever and the engine stopped. "Foreigners, eh?" he said. "Where are you from?"

"We are English," I said. "My friend and I are travelling to Bucharest on a mission of great importance."

"Hello, Englishmen. I am Florin. I will take you to Orsova. There you will get a train to Craiova, then to Bucharest. Jump up please."

After three hours the huge engine rattled onto the streets of Orsova. Fortunately the town had a well-established railway station. After thanking Florin for his kindness, Holmes purchased the tickets with some of the Lei, the Roumanian currency, which Zoltan had acquired for us from Kurach.

The Craiova train was in the station, so we waited in the sunshine for the whistle which would announce its departure. I opened my haversack to see what edible contents Zoltan had packed. As I sifted through the comestibles my hand fell upon something disc-shaped and metallic. I extracted this strange object and held it up for inspection. "Look at this, Holmes," I said.

Holmes took the disc from me and looked at it.

"It is some kind of emblem. That is undoubtedly a death's head. The letters are of the Cyrillic alphabet and it has a rosette and ribbon of blue, red and white."

"What do you make of it?"

"Unless I am very wrong, this is the emblem of a secret organisation, 'Unity or Death', otherwise known as 'The Black Hand'."

"Good heavens," I cried. "This must be the object Milan held up in his palm several times during our journey through Serbia and Montenegro."

"Look at this, Watson. There is a note pinned to the reverse of the ribbon. "Here." He held out the emblem for my inspection. I looked at the note. It was from Milan and it read:

'Good luck, Dr. Watson. Think of me sometimes.'

I have to say that this little gift left me very moved.

The journey to Bucharest proved to be long but uneventful. At the central station Holmes approached a policeman and asked if he could recommend suitable lodgings. The officer's French was not good, so he called out to a tall, distinguished man of perhaps forty years, for assistance. He approached us smiling.

"You are seeking accommodation? I am sorry but there is little to be had around here. For how long do you wish to stay?"

"We need lodgings for one night only." Holmes said.

"My friend and I are on an urgent mission. Perhaps you have heard of us. I am Sherlock Holmes. This is Dr. Watson."

Holmes held out his documents. The man carefully scrutinised them. He held out his hand. "Welcome to Bucharest, gentlemen. I am Illie Ionescu, the local magistrate. Perhaps you would care to stay the night with my wife and me?"

Supper was over and we had retired for a pipe and a glass of Slivowitz, a delicious plum brandy popular in the region. Mr. Ionescu leaned back in his chair and puffed contentedly at his pipe.

"Well now, gentlemen," he said. "How do you find my country?"

Holmes looked keenly at our host. "I find it most interesting and remarkable."

"It is not the backward region that you perhaps were expecting?"

"No, indeed. It is quite refreshing to discover such a centre of enlightenment." Holmes glanced in my direction. "Do you not agree, Doctor?"

"Undoubtedly," I said. "After journeying through countries which seem to be little more than the personal fiefdoms of cut-throats and bandits, it comes as a distinct pleasure to discover such an oasis of culture."

Mr. Ionescu bowed his head in acknowledgement.

"Thank you, Dr. Watson. We Roumanians are proud of our nationalism and our internationalism." And he proceeded to tell us something of the history of Roumania.

*****

Our host reached once more for the coffeepot and was about to refill our cups, when there came the sound of the doorbell being pulled frantically. Mr. Ionescu looked at the long case clock in the corner by the doorway and sighed.

"It is after ten. A casual caller would not arrive so late, so there must be something amiss."

Sherlock Holmes and I looked quizzically at each other. Mr. Ionescu, observing our puzzled expressions, smiled as he stood up.

"As a part of my magisterial duties, I am also an officer of the law and occasionally a coroner. When matters arise, that the local constabulary cannot fathom, or when someone dies in a manner which may be regarded as unusual, then I am called on for advice and assistance."

The bell rang again, more loudly. He sighed again. "I had better answer the door, before our visitor wakes the children."

A few moments later, our host returned. With him was a tall, well-built man in his thirties. He was clean-shaven and his square jaw line and strong mouth gave the impression of a man who knew his own mind. It had evidently been raining, for he shook his hat and a light shower of water was dislodged.

For several minutes, Mr. Ionescu and the newcomer conversed in Roumanian. Then he turned and addressed Holmes and myself in French once more. "It is as I imagined, gentlemen. Mr. Lupescu the senior police officer for this district. I suppose that, in England you would rank him an inspector. He has just brought me news of a most interesting case." Once more he turned to the policeman. Continuing to speak in French, he said. "Mr. Lupescu. Perhaps you would care to repeat your information to my honoured guests, Mr. Sherlock Holmes and Dr. Watson, of Baker Street, England?"

The Inspector looked at us in some disbelief. "You are truly Mr. Holmes and Dr. Watson? I have heard much about your celebrated cases. Indeed, who has not? If you are willing, then you may greatly assist me in a matter that deeply perplexes and worries me."

Holmes stood up and held out his hand. "I am Holmes, if I may be of any assistance, you have only to ask it of me."

Mr. Lupescu threw his hat onto the desk and sat heavily into the vacant chair by the fire. He sighed. "Mr. Holmes, tonight I have attended the scene of a most dreadful crime, in which a young man appears to have shot and killed his own father in a fit of alcoholic rage. The young man swears his innocence, but he was alone with his father in a locked room when the murder took place … and yet."

Sherlock Holmes sat in the chair opposite to the policeman and looked keenly at him. "Now, Mr. Lupescu. If we take this matter slowly and carefully, perhaps we may reach a firm judgement. Now, sir, please tell me the complete story."

Mr. Lupescu drew a heavy sigh and gratefully accepted the brandy offered to him by our host. "It was at six-thirty when I received a message from the local constable that something dreadful had occurred at the house of Mr. Prodan, the railway proprietor." He took a sip at his drink then continued.

"It took me half an hour to reach his house, which is situated at the edge of the city and when I arrived, I found the place in a dreadful turmoil. According to the coachman, who opened the door to me, Mr. Prodan had been shot and killed by none other than his son, Nicolai. The young man had come home at about six o'clock in the evening. He was, even at this early hour, very drunk. Nicholai had evidently been drinking for some hours with his friends in Bucharest and had come home to borrow money from his father so he could continue to make merry. Something, I understand, he had done many times before.

"When he arrived, Nicolai was extremely abusive to Jacob, the footman who answered the door. Staggering towards his father's study, he stopped only to swear at Mr. Klein, the old man's secretary, before taking the key from the lock and locking both his father and himself in the study."

"For a while there was little to be heard, then all of a sudden angry voices could be heard from behind the door. Mr. Prodan was heard to say: "You have disgraced the family name once too often, Nicholai. If you desire any more money, you will have to go out and earn it for yourself. You will not have another penny out of me!"

"Then Nicolai's voice could be heard, more pleading than angry. 'Please, father. Just this once, I beg you. It is a debt of honour'.

"But his father was not to be persuaded. 'You will have to face the consequences of your actions!' he cried. To which his son angrily replied 'I could kill you, old man'. Then there came the sound of a struggle and of furniture falling over, and suddenly the sound of a shot. Then silence.

"If the argument had been heard all over the house, it was the sound of gunfire which followed galvanised the inhabitants. Mrs. Prodan came down from her bedroom, the cook and the maids from the kitchen and Mr. Klein emerged from the library, next door to Mr. Prodan's study.

"Klein was the first to react. 'The key, where is the key?' Jacob reminded the secretary that Nicolai had taken the key and locked the door from the inside. Klein peered through the keyhole only to discover that the key was missing. Mrs. Prodan cried out to him that he should force the door. Klein, however, said that the door was too heavy and the lock too well constructed to force. He would go back into the library, climb through the window and see if he might force an entry through the French window in the study.

"A few minutes later, they could hear the sound of breaking glass followed swiftly by the key being turned in the lock. The scene that met their eyes was one of considerable destruction. The room looked as if it had been struck by a whirlwind. Young Nicolai was slumped in an armchair by the window, seemingly quite oblivious to the world. On the hearthrug lay the twisted body of Mr. Prodan. He had been shot in the chest and lay in a crimson pool of his own blood.

"At the sight of her dead husband, Mrs. Prodan became quite hysterical and had to be led away by the cook and one of the maids. It was then that attention fell upon Nicolai. Jacob took Klein's arm and pointed to the young man, who, despite the uproar, had moved not a muscle. It appeared as if the alcohol he had absorbed had drained him of all his powers of movement. Then, in his hand, they noticed a gun.

No greater evidence of the young man's guilt could possibly exist, Mr. Holmes."

Sherlock Holmes looked sharply at the Inspector. "Do not be too quick to assume the obvious," he said.

Mr. Lupescu sighed. "It is the precise conclusion to which I myself have come, sir. Nicholai, when questioned about the matter, freely admitted to the argument and the unpleasantness that had followed it. He and his father had come to blows. Mr. Prodan, being a large and active man, despite his advanced years, had landed a heavy blow to the young man's head, which for a few seconds had stunned him. He fell into the armchair where Klein and Jacob had found him. The effects of the blow, combined with the alcohol he had drunk earlier, had been sufficient to cause him to pass out temporarily. He had heard the sound of a gunshot and when he came to himself, he realised that the gun had somehow found its way into his hands. Yet he swears it was not he who shot his father. He is so earnest, Mr. Holmes. But it has to be Nicholai, for no other person was present when the murder took place."

Mr. Lupescu looked intently at Sherlock Holmes. "Tonight, I came here to seek the advice of Mr. Ionescu. But now that I find you, Mr. Holmes, Europe's greatest detective in his house, I beg you to look into this matter and find out the exact truth."

Sherlock Holmes looked thoughtfully at the policeman. "Do you believe that Nicolai Prodan shot and killed his father, Inspector?"

"I do not know what to believe, Mr. Holmes. All the evidence points to his guilt. Yet in the face of all this, he remains steadfast in his protestation of innocence. Perhaps a third party was responsible, but I cannot see how …" He shook his head. "No, Nicholai, must be guilty."

Holmes stood up and stretched himself up to his full height. His eyes were gleaming. "Well now, Mr. Lupescu," he said smiling. "If you require my assistance, then you shall have it. What do you say, Watson?"

"My dear fellow, it will be quite like old times."

Holmes took up Mr. Lupescu's hat and held it out to him. "Come along, Inspector. The game's afoot and time is wasting."

*****

It was almost eleven o'clock, when at last our carriage drew up beside the large wrought iron gates of the house of Prodan. The rain had given away to light drizzle and such light as there was, was reflected on the wet streets.

Mr. Lupescu stepped down and called out; a uniformed man opened the gates.

Mr. Lupescu stepped aboard once more and the carriage lurched forward. Then we found ourselves in the grounds of the residence. As we approached the house it was plain to see that the residents had yet to go to their beds for the property was a blaze of light; little wonder, I mused, after experiencing such a terrible experience as a brutal murder.

In the hallway we were received by Mr. Prodan's coachman, Tomas. Tomas said nothing, he merely ushered Mr. Ionescu, Holmes and myself into a well appointed sitting room. Mr. Lupescu led away. I looked around the room and noticed with approval that the décor would have done justice to the most noble household in England.

"This is a very fine house, indeed," I remarked.

Mr. Ionescu warmed himself by the fire. "The house was once the property of a Boier family, one of the 'Mosierime', the landlords of much of our lands. The house and indeed much of their estates, were leased to Mr. Prodan several years ago. Like so many of their class, the family took little interest in the lands they owned and as so many have done, they are now living in Paris."

The arrival of a tall, dark-haired man in his late thirties interrupted him. The look of acute sadness in the newcomer's eyes quickly reminded us of the tragic nature of our errand. To my surprise he addressed us in flawless English. "Good evening, gentlemen. I am Rudolf Klein, Mr. Prodan's secretary. Mr. Lupescu informs me that we are honoured by the presence of Mr. Sherlock Holmes and Dr. Watson. The family will be greatly relieved to discover that such dignified figures as yourselves are investigating. Although it appears to be an open and shut case, nevertheless."

The greeting, although cordial and effusive, left me with the distinct impression that it was a welcome tinged with disapproval.

Holmes stepped forward and identified himself. "Thank you, sir. I am Holmes. Could you show us the body?"

As we entered the study the body of the late Mr. Prodan was still to be seen lying on the hearthrug. The corpse, however, had been partially covered with a tablecloth, but the red stain of blood could still be plainly observed.

I looked around the room. It was large and decorated with equally large and expensive furnishings and hanging tapestries. The tall windows and French doors leading to the garden were hung with, huge velvet curtains. One of the windows was open, for the cool night air was blowing the curtains quite rhythmically in a silent and tuneless dance.

At once, Sherlock Holmes was transformed. No longer was he the languid, almost disinterested figure. He was now almost cat-like in his movements. For a short time he scrambled about the floor, his eyes ceaselessly searching the room for clues and snippets of information. Abruptly he stood up.

"Watson, I believe a early inspection of the body would be in order." He pulled back the cloth to reveal the head and shoulders of the dead man. Mr. Prodan lay there with a look of complete surprise on his face. He was clothed in a dressing gown, a shirt, trousers and slippers. "Well, now, Doctor. What do you make of it?"

I ran my hand down the dressing gown and untied the cord. Pulling it back a little I observed a small hole in the chest just below the heart. "Hmm …" I mused. "This is clearly where the bullet entered the body, Holmes." Taking a firm grasp of his shoulder, I half turned Mr. Prodan's body. The exit hole was both large and bloody. "Here is were the bullet emerged. Although I have to say that it is a little lower than at first I would have imagined."

Holmes stopped his examination of the window and came over to join me. He crouched down beside me and closely observed the corpse. "Please explain yourself, Watson," he said.

"Well, Nicolai is quite a tall young man according to Mr. Lupescu. If he had fired at his father's chest from a standing position, I would have expected the exit hole to have been somewhat lower and if he had fired from a seated position it should have been much higher. Yet the exit hole is virtually parallel to the entry hole."

Holmes smiled and nodded. "Thank you, Doctor, your remarks have proved to be most illuminating and instructive."

"Here is the gun," said Mr. Lupescu. "It is of a foreign make, a Luger, I believe." He depressed the handle and released the clip. "Ah, yes, one round has been fired."

"Indeed," Holmes nodded. "If we seek for it I confidently expect the bullet will be found somewhere adjacent to the fireplace." He glanced in my direction. "Watson, perhaps you would be kind enough to begin the search."

"Certainly, Holmes," I replied.

And whilst I poked around the fireplace and inspected the walls, Sherlock Holmes continued his examination of the window. Then he lightly stepped through the open void and into the garden. A few moments later he returned nodding to himself and briskly rubbing his hands together.

"Now, Inspector, I desire to speak with the members of the household. I trust that you have made appropriate arrangements?"

Mr. Lupescu nodded. "Certainly, sir. I believe that Mr. Ionescu is at this very moment organising everybody."

To my relief all but the youngest housemaid spoke good French. Nicolai was the first to be interviewed by Holmes. He was a tall, handsome young man with a dark, rather sulky face, and was still dressed in his town clothes. He also had, I noticed, beginnings of a large bruise on his left cheek.

Mr. Lupescu sat the young man down opposite Holmes and myself. "This is Mr. Sherlock Holmes, the great English detective. Answer him truthfully. If, as you claim, you are innocent, Mr. Holmes will surely assist you."

For the next few minutes Holmes questioned the young man who to my mind answered fully and truthfully. He had indeed arrived home considerably the worse for drink and had picked a violent quarrel with his father over money, something that had occurred on several previous occasions. He admitted that on this occasion the argument had boiled over into violence when his father had struck him on the cheek.

Holmes carefully observed the young man. "Did you then take up one of the guns I see festooning the study and, in a fit of temper, shoot your father?"

Nicolai shook his head and sighed deeply. "Mr. Holmes, I have to tell you that I do not really know. The effects of the alcohol, combined with the hard blow given to me by my father, left me in quite a daze; and I cannot in all frankness remember anything until Klein and Jacob dragged me out into the corridor."

Holmes glanced across to me and frowned. He stood up. "Very well, thank you, Nicolai. I will speak with you again later."

Mr. Lupescu stood up and quietly ushered the young man from the room.

"Holmes," I said urgently. "I believe that Nicolai by his uncertainty is virtually signing his own death warrant, and unless you can furnish the authorities with an alternative suspect he may be facing the rope?"

Sherlock Holmes bit his lip in a gesture of frustration.

"I know it, Doctor," he replied. "But I have hope that such tiny pieces of evidence that exist in and around Mr. Prodan's study may yet assist us in getting to the heart of the matter."

I smiled to myself. This was Holmes at his most enigmatic. I was unable to follow up his remarks with questions, however, because Mrs. Prodan was standing before me.

The lady was tall and handsome. It was clear to me from whom Nicolai had inherited his looks. She had been crying and her eyes were still quite red.

Holmes stood up and held out his hand. "Mrs. Prodan. I am Sherlock Holmes, Mr. Lupescu has asked me to assist him. Can you tell me the exact nature of the events that took place tonight?"

"Well, sir," said the lady slowly. "I was upstairs in my dressing room, when Nicolai came home. I was about to retire and Katrina, one of our maids was assisting me. I did not hear my son come in, but very soon, I was aware of another argument between my husband and my son. Then there came the sound of a gunshot." At this juncture, the lady began to weep and it was some time before she was sufficiently composed to continue. "When we heard the shot, Katrina and I immediately made our way downstairs.

"As we reached the top of the main stairs I looked over the balcony and saw Cora the cook, Elisabet and Jacob at the top of the service stairs. Then Mr. Klein came out of the library and shouted for a key to the study door."

Holmes frowned. "The key was not in the lock?"

"No. Nicolai must have taken it and locked his father and himself in the study."

"Are spare keys kept in the house?"

"Yes, Jacob was sent downstairs to the kitchen to look for the spare key, but he came back empty-handed."

Holmes frowned once more, and nodded, but he made no comment, but clearly something had registered in his quick mind. "Thank you, Mrs. Prodan, that is extremely informative, please continue."

"Mr. Klein banged on the door and called out to my husband and Nicholai, but to no avail. Jacob suggested that they should break down the door, but Mr. Klein had a better idea. He would try and gain entry through the garden. A few moments later, we heard the breaking glass, then the key being turned in the lock," Mrs. Prodan broke into a sob. "Then I saw my dear husband, dead on the floor."

Mr. Lupescu placed a comforting arm around the lady's shoulder. "Thank you, Mrs. Prodan," he said. He gave Holmes a questioning look. Holmes nodded his assent and the Policeman led the distraught lady away.

The household staff were quickly interviewed one by one and there emerged little difference in their telling accounts of the events. Only the cook seemed to be at odds with them. "It was the *sound* of the gunshot, Mr. Holmes."

"The sound? Please explain."

"Yes, sir. It didn't sound quite loud enough, if you take my meaning. It was a little muffled."

"How do you mean, muffled?" I said.

"Well, sir. When I was a girl, I lived in the little town of Arad, where we used to go hunting quite a lot and I fancy I know when a shot has been muffled."

When the good lady had gone, I looked from Holmes to Mr. Lupescu. The Policeman seemed baffled; but in Holmes's eye I detected a definite gleam. Then Mr. Lupescu snapped his fingers. "Perhaps the gun was fired through a cushion to muffle the noise," he said. "We will have to inspect them to see if it is so."

Holmes smiled. "Indeed, Inspector. Perhaps we should. But we should interview Mr. Klein first."

The policeman nodded and once more left the library. I glanced at Holmes. He was chuckling quietly.

"Holmes, the very idea of a cushion being employed to deaden the sound of gunfire seems to amuse you. Have I missed something?"

Holmes reached out and slapped me heartily on the knee. "No, old fellow. It is something I have just understood when it is added to the small shreds of evidence I earlier observed. I was laughing at my slowness in coming to the correct judgement."

"You have solved the case," I spluttered in frank amazement.

"Not yet, Watson, but I now see in which direction the evidence is leading me. We shall see, old fellow, we shall see."

The library door opened once more. It was Mr. Klein. His dark eyes swiftly travelled around the room and over the faces of Holmes and myself. Once more the conversation was held in English.

"Now, sir," said Holmes, as the secretary took his seat. "You were here in the library when the shot was fired?"

Klein nodded. "That is so, Mr. Holmes, I had just completed my monthly accounts and was about to go into Mr. Prodan's study and enquire if he needed me further tonight."

"You overheard the argument between father and son?"

"Indeed, who did not?"

"It was a violent argument?"

"Yes, I heard the old man shout at his son that he would have no more money and that he should get out of his house. Then a fierce struggle began, I could hear furniture being knocked over. Then a shot rang out and there was silence."

Holmes looked carefully at the Austrian. "Where were you standing when the shot was fired, Mr. Klein?"

Klein looked slightly abashed. "I have a small confession to make, Mr. Holmes. I was standing at the window enjoying an illicit cigarette. You see, Mrs. Prodan does not approve of smoking in the house and ordinarily I wait until I have reached the sanctity of my room. Tonight, however, the heavy workload, and the vile unpleasantness I had encountered at the hands of Mr. Nicolai, had strained my nerves somewhat, so I opened the window and lit a cigarette. It was the sound of the gunshot which interrupted my smoking."

"Ah, yes. The gunshot," said Holmes. "What exactly did you do when you heard it, Mr. Klein?"

The secretary knitted his brows in thought for a moment. "I threw the cigarette out into the garden. I closed the window and ran into the hall where the other members of the household were gathering."

Holmes nodded. "Very good." He stood up and walked casually over to the window. "What did you do next?"

Mr. Klein stood up also and followed Holmes over to the window. "The door to Mr. Prodan's study was locked and the spare key could not be found. I quickly realised that breaking down the door was not an option, so I returned to the library in order to get into the study through the French windows.

"Once more, I threw open the window, then whilst I was half way through, I realised that I should need something to break the glass and get in. So I returned, picked up a heavy paperweight from the desk. Then I ran along the little path which circles the house to Mr. Prodan's study.

"It took me only a moment to look through the window and see that Mr. Prodan was lying on the floor and that Mr. Nicolai was slumped in a chair. I smashed the glass in the window, reached in and released the catch. Then I opened the window, climbed in and ran to the study door. The key I found on the floor near to the chair in which Mr. Nicolai sat."

"Did you not stop to examine the two men?" I asked.

"No, sir. I did not," said Klein emphatically. "Even the most casual observer would have perceived that Mr. Prodan was dead and that Mr. Nicolai was too stupefied to move."

Holmes smiled. "Excellent, Mr. Klein. Your description of tonight's events is most clear." He turned to Mr. Lupescu. "Inspector, we require some lights for the next part of our investigation."

"Lights?" said the policeman, plainly surprised by the request.

"Indeed, if we are to stage a reconstruction, they will be most useful."

The Policeman frowned. He seemed doubtful. "If you think it necessary, Mr. Holmes," he said. "My men are waiting at headquarters for permission to take away Mr. Prodan's body. I will ask for lamps to be brought with them."

Mr. Lupescu ushered Klein out of the library. As the door closed behind them, I grasped Holmes by the arm.

"It is your intention to begin a reconstruction at this hour?"

Holmes nodded. "There are one or two points of interest which have surfaced that may be as illuminating as the lighting if we reconstruct, Watson. For the present, however, I shall say no more."

*****

The midnight hour was almost upon us before Sherlock Holmes was ready to begin. He had informed the members of the household of his intentions and that they were expected to take up their positions and act exactly as they had earlier.

When all was ready, Holmes, Mr. Lupescu and Mr. Ionescu took up various positions in the hall. As the body of Mr. Prodan had been removed, it was none other than John Watson MD (retired) who was given the single honour of replacing him (without similar fatal consequences, I sincerely hoped). A policeman's rattle had been substituted for the gun and was to be employed at the critical moment.

At a signal from Mr. Lupescu, I entered the study and closed the door. The tableau then commenced. Nicolai Prodan entered the house and quickly joined me in the study. The young man was quite pale and looked completely washed out. He was able to mutter some barely coherent sentences before I took up the rattle and agitated it briskly.

Suddenly the French doors burst open. There stood the figure of Sherlock Holmes. Somehow he had slipped out quite unnoticed into the garden.

"Holmes," I cried. "What is happening?"

He held up a small brass object in one hand; then in the other he produced a large key. "We have our killer, Watson," he said. Then, turning to address two shadowy figures lurking in the semi-darkness of the garden, he snapped. "Do we not, Mr. Klein?"

"Klein?" I spluttered. "He is the culprit?"

The figures moved out of the darkness and into the light. One was indeed Klein. The other, a large uniformed figure, held the Austrian tightly by the arm.

An angry flush spread across the face of young Nicolai.

"You swine," he cried, lashing out at the secretary. "I'll kill you!"

It was only the intervention of Holmes and Mr. Ionescu that prevented Nicolai from assaulting Klein. They securely grasped him by the arms and propelled him to a vacant chair. He glared at Sherlock Holmes. "Why do you stop me? This swine has killed my father and almost succeeded in placing my head in a noose."

"Swine, eh?" yelled the Austrian. Klein struggled fiercely and almost broke free from the grip of his captor. Killing your father was a pleasure, my only regret is I could not succeed in killing you too."

For a moment, it seemed as if another fight might break out in the study. Then Holmes banged the flat of his hand on the desk. "Silence," he cried.

"Now," he said evenly, looking at the two would be combatants. "Let us get to the heart of the matter. Mr. Klein, your crime was one of malice and forethought. Revenge for slights, real or imagined. Perhaps you will now be kind enough to enlighten us?"

Klein, pale and drawn, gazed at Nicolai with ill-disguised contempt. He was clearly suffering from great emotion, yet his voice remained both steady and clear.

"Six years ago, I was working in Vienna, for a firm which was arranging finance for Mr. Prodan. I had access to the firm's money. I was trusted, respected.

One day I learned that my father was extremely ill, he needed a complicated and expensive operation. I ... I borrowed some of the firm's money."

"It was embezzlement!" cried Nicolai.

Klein nodded and sighed deeply. "I admit it, Mr. Holmes. It was embezzlement."

"But why did you not approach the company's partners, surely they would have helped you?" I asked.

"I did not think they would agree, the sum needed amounted to almost a year's salary. They would have said no, I am sure."

"Was the treatment successful, Mr. Klein?" asked Sherlock Holmes.

Klein sighed again. "No, sir. I am afraid it was not. I had taken a grave risk for nothing." He shook his head. "Then Mr. Prodan came to see me. He said that he knew all about the missing money. Well I explained myself and begged him not to turn me over to the authorities because I would pay back every penny I had taken.

"Well, Mr. Holmes you may find it strange, but Mr. Prodan just laughed. He said that I should not concern myself. He would repay the money, and in return I would return with him to Roumania, as his secretary."

Sherlock Holmes smiled his thin smile. "So you came to Bucharest to assist Mr. Prodan?"

"Yes, sir, but he treated me vilely, as did his coward of a son. Every menial task was given to me … and I was insulted every day. Not merely about my crime, but vile sacrilegious remarks about my religion, everything."

For a brief moment my eyes wandered away from the young Austrian and onto the form of Nicolai Prodan. It was in that instant, I knew the tale was exactly true. Nicolai seemed to have shrunk in his seat. His eyes now bore the dull lifeless look of a man who has heard the truth and is shaken by it. I was puzzled, however, by Klein's passivity. "But, Mr. Klein why did you not return to Vienna instead of remaining in Bucharest, only to suffer further indignities. Indeed, you seemed like a fly to be blundering into the spider's web. Besides, Mr. Prodan was also implicated in the concealment of a crime, how could he then hurt you?"

Klein smiled a bitter smile. "You would judge that to be true, Dr. Watson, would you not? Things were not so simple, however. You are correct. In law, he was as guilty as I, but he still held a trump card in his hand. He simply threatened that if I didn't comply with his wishes, he would ensure that my mother would be informed of my crime. So soon after my father's death, I knew that she would take it very badly indeed as she was not in good health herself. I believed that any such revelation would surely kill her."

Sherlock Holmes nodded. "But, as I have said, you have waited for so long to extract your revenge. What is it that has come about in your circumstances which has made it possible for you to openly take action? If I am not mistaken it is your mother, Mr. Klein, is it not? She has recently died."

Sherlock Holmes and the Bolshevik Plot

The Austrian nodded his face was grim. "Indeed, Mr. Holmes. It was last week when I received a letter from a cousin telling me of my mother's passing. Her health had given out."

"For a moment I was sad, but I quickly realised that my crimes could no longer hurt her. It was time for my revenge on two wicked men, who deserved fulsome retribution. My only regret is that Nicolai Prodan is still alive."

The young man stood up and turned towards his captors. "Come along, Mr. Lupescu. It is time to do your duty. Take me away, I do not wish to stay a moment longer in this dreadful house."

So saying, the young man saluted the assembly and disappeared with the policeman into the night air.

*****

It was after 2 a.m. when Sherlock Holmes, Mr. Ionescu and myself found ourselves rattling through the deserted streets of Bucharest, once more. The rain, fortunately absent during our investigation, now returned with will full vigour.

The terrible events of the evening had clearly made a strong impression on Mr. Ionescu and he felt a strong and understandable desire to discuss the matter. "It was a fine piece of work, Mr. Holmes, uncovering the real culprit," he said.

Holmes looked keenly at our host. "It is all a matter of opinion, Mr. Ionescu, in this particular case, who is the victim and who is the culprit?" he said.

Mr. Ionescu sat up very straight in his seat, his face bore a startled look. "Mr. Holmes!" he said.

There was a short silence in the carriage before Mr. Ionescu spoke again. "It is all very well for you, Mr. Holmes. A man who stands aloof, dispensing his own justice as he sees fit. But for the good of the majority, crime is crime and what ever form it takes, it must be accounted for and a suitable punishment handed down. Society demands nothing less.

Even as a liberal, I cannot subscribe to your well published opinions."

For the briefest of moments, Holmes looked keenly at Mr. Ionescu. Then he broke into a loud laugh. "Watson, I am discovered. Even in Roumania your accounts of my activities have laid bare all too clearly my personal views on malefactors and their punishment." He turned to Mr. Ionescu. "My dear, sir, I am unable to subscribe to the official view that crime and punishment hold a fixed dominion over each other. They do not. Each case is as individual and distinctive as the fingerprints on each hand. From the look on your face, I see that we shall have to agree to disagree on the matter."

Keen to avoid further argument and possible conflict between my friend and our host, I swiftly turned to the way in which Holmes had unmasked Klein.

"You will doubtless recall, Doctor, that as is my wont in these matters, I took great interest in the study floor?"

Mr. Ionescu laughed at the memory. "I have to confess, Mr. Holmes, it was something of a shock to observe you scrambling around on all fours, even though Dr. Watson's excellent publications have warned me that it should occur. But what did you discover, which indicated to you that the culprit was not Nicolai but Klein?"

Holmes reached into his waistcoat pocket and held up a small brass object. "Why, it is the spent cartridge case you produced earlier," I said.

"Indeed," said Holmes. "Fired from the gun discovered in the hands of young Nicolai. Yet despite the close relationship between them they were not to be found in the same room."

"Good heavens," I cried. "Then where did you find it, Holmes?"

"Presently, Watson," he said smiling. "Let us immediately turn to your own observations. You stated that the bullet had apparently entered Mr. Prodan's body at the wrong angle?"

"Exactly," I agreed. "Nicolai is a tall young man and the only way he could have shot his father in such a way was by standing on the desk."

"Or at a greater distance than originally contemplated?"

"Yes, but all the evidence points to Nicolai and his father never being further than a few feet apart. If we are to take your view then Mr. Prodan was shot from several feet, maybe twenty."

Holmes smiled triumphantly. "Then would it surprise you, my dear Watson, if I informed you that I discovered the cartridge case in the garden?"

"Then the gun was not fired by Nicolai, but by another hand."

"Excellent, Watson. We progress. Now, what of the position of the corpse?"

"The man lay on his back as if punched and knocked down," I said cautiously.

"Exactly," said Holmes emphatically. "If a man had been hit at close range by a large calibre bullet he would have been sent spinning. It follows therefore, that he was shot from some distance."

"The garden?"

"Indeed."

"Then it would also explain why the cook described the sound of the gunshot as muffled."

I was curious to understand exactly how Holmes had concluded that it was Klein, and not Nicolai who had fired the fatal shot. He was unequivocal in his reply. "Well now, Watson. Perhaps I should initially describe Klein's *modus operandi*. Not for the first time did he overhear a violent argument between the two Prodans. On this occasion, however, Klein, possessed the wherewithal to destroy them both; now that his beloved mother had passed over to a plane where the machinations of humanity could no longer wound her, he used the situation for his own ends and advantage.

"Nicolai had arrived in a foul temper, drunk almost to the point of incapacity. He roundly abused Klein and almost immediately became involved in a heated argument with his father. As the argument degenerated into an altercation, Klein seized the moment. Taking up his pistol he had carefully prepared for such an occasion, Klein opened the library window. He stepped out into the garden and edged a little cautiously along the little pathway. Peering in through the high casement window into the study, Klein observed the ferocious fistfight between the two men. Careful not to step into the light, he took his pistol, aimed it at the old man and fired.

"He wanted long enough to see the body of Mr. Prodan fall to the floor, then he returned to the library as quickly as possible. A few moments later he opened the library door and stepped into the midst of an excited crowd of household staff.

"When it was discovered that the door to Prodan's study was locked, Klein immediately volunteered to gain entrance through the garden door. I am sure he did not wish to have the door broken down. Stopping only to collect a large paperweight, he returned to the exact spot he had so recently vacated outside the casement window. He smashed the window with the paperweight and opened the window catch, then he stepped in.

"Seeing Nicolai slumped in the chair in a semi-comatose state, Klein, hardly believing his good fortune, slipped the gun into the young man's hands. He then opened the study door and revealed to the world a case of patricide."

Mr. Ionescu nodded vigorously. "You are undoubtedly right, Mr. Holmes. But what I do not understand is how you were able to uncover the matter."

"As soon as the fact that Nicolai was not the culprit became clear to me, it was a matter of deducing who had pulled the trigger. Klein was my immediate suspect. He alone had no one with him when the shot was fired. I also asked myself why should he smash the casement window, when the door to the garden had the key in the lock, unless, of course, it was to obliterate all trace of the bullet hole.

"That is why he took with him such a large and heavy object with which to break the glass," I said, "when, under normal circumstances, a stone, or indeed the heel of his shoe would have been a more appropriate tool."

Holmes nodded. "It was the matter of shoes which gave me the final piece of the jigsaw. If Klein had made only one journey between the library and the study only one set of footprints should have existed. Yet my observations showed me that there in the wet earth, there were two. Clearly someone had made the journey twice. I had no doubt, therefore, that Klein was my man."

Four

The morning sun had risen into a bright clear sky. All signs of the previous night's rain had vanished, save a few puddles on the roadway. Sherlock Holmes and Mr. Ionescu were putting on their hats and coats. Refreshed by even the shortest night's sleep, Holmes was eager to see something of the city.

"I believe you will like Bucharest very much, Mr. Holmes," said our host. "It has been called 'the Paris of the Balkans' by those who know about such matters."

His children were also dressed and ready to depart. Mr. Ionescu was taking them to school and they were jumping around his legs in a most animated fashion. "It is almost Easter," he explained. "The children are very excited about preparing something at school for their mother."

For myself, I had decided to remain indoors, for the first part of the day at least. The constant travelling, allied to the damp and cold conditions we had suffered, during the latter part of our journey, had brought back my old aches and pains. As a consequence, I prescribed complete rest for myself.

Feeling at something of a loose end, I wandered casually into the garden. It was a jolly little place and quite unlike any English garden. I sat on a bench placed conveniently close to the back door and took out my pipe. The sun by now had warmed the air somewhat and it felt quite pleasant and relaxing to sit quietly for a time and relegate our quest and the future to the back of my mind.

"Dr. Watson. I believe you may have need of these." It was Mrs. Ionescu. She was holding out my Vesta case.

I stood up. "Thank you, will you not join me in enjoying this excellent morning ... supposing you do not dislike the pipe?"

The lady sat down upon the bench and gestured for me to join her there.

We began to speak of conditions in Roumania.

I asked, "How has the recent Balkan war affected Roumania?"

"When the conflict began last October it was the King's decision to remain neutral. Then the combined assault of Serbia, Bulgaria, Greece and Montenegro virtually overwhelmed Turkey and she was forced to sue for peace. Her power in the region is all but broken. Now we have to organise ourselves. The material is all about us. All we need is patience and determination."

"Indeed," I agreed. "But do not forget, Rome, as the poet said, was not built in a day. You should prepare yourself for further conflict. Serbia will not be content until all foreign interference is cleared out of the Balkans, and Austria and Turkey are still very much in evidence here."

The kitchen door opened and there stood our host, he was wreathed in smiles. "There you are, Dr. Watson. I hope you are rested?"

"Indeed, I am, sir," I said, standing to greet him.

Mr. Ionescu sat down on the bench and blew out his cheeks. "I have been making enquiries on your behalf about the Russians who have abducted your Mr. Andrews," he said. "None of the officials or their informants in Bucharest have any news of them. As you know, Dr. Watson, Russians are not exactly welcome here in Roumania. If any have passed through the city, I have no doubt that they would have been observed."

I frowned. This was most odd. It was a pity that Sherlock Holmes was not present to consider the matter. I questioned Mr. Ionescu further. "How could they make their way to St. Petersburg, if not through Roumania?"

"They have undoubtedly travelled along the Danube," said a familiar, but disembodied, voice.

"Holmes, where are you?" I cried.

The head and shoulders of my friend and colleague appeared above the garden gate. He leaned over and unlatched it. Mr. Ionescu gestured for Holmes to come and sit down. "Mr. Holmes is correct, Dr. Watson. As far as I can judge the matter, when they left Belgrade, they would not have travelled through Hungary or Transylvania, as both must be regarded by them as enemy territory. The Danube appears to be the only avenue open to them."

Mrs. Ionescu, who had disappeared at the outset of our conversation, now reappeared carrying a large tray piled high with freshly baked bread, cheese, dried fruit and coffee.

After we had eaten, Holmes and I discussed with our host the no little matter of our journey. A train leaving for Ploiesta, some thirty-five miles North of Bucharest, was due to depart at two o'clock that afternoon. From this staging post Holmes and I were to travel to the Ukranian border via Bazau and Burcau, crossing the border near the small town of Siret. Allowing for an overnight stop in Burcau, we would take approximately twenty-four hours to reach our immediate destination of Chernovtsy. I took out my watch and sighed. It was past noon, presently we would be leaving this pleasant idyll and once more facing the unknown. It was a prospect to which I looked forward with scant anticipation. Holmes was no more enthusiastic.

"Indeed, I understand, Watson, here in Romania we have found something to tarry for. All things, however, must come to an end, be they good or evil." He stood up. "Mrs. Ionescu has volunteered to escort me around the local provision store where, apparently, they also sell a line of sturdy outdoor apparel."

I looked at my jacket and trousers and nodded. The second-hand clothing we had purchased in Montenegro had scarcely been of premier quality when new; it was by now looking distinctly threadbare.

"I believe I shall order something in tweed. Plus fours perhaps, eh, Watson?" Holmes continued.

"Please do not purchase anything that would make us stand out in a crowd," I protested.

Mr. Ionescu chuckled. "I do not think that you have much to worry yourself about, Dr. Watson. The road to Kiev is populated with many and varied people. As a positive Mecca for the world's traders, you will meet folk of all manner of dress."

"Well that is as may be," I objected. "But I have no desire to arrive in Kiev dressed in anything outlandish."

Holmes looked at me with a serious face. "Now that, my dear fellow, is a pity. For I had intended that we should turn up in front of the Patriarch dressed as Barbary pirates."

It was a little before the hour of two when we arrived once again at the impressive central station. Mr. Ionescu had accompanied Holmes and myself to the platform where the Ploiesti train stood steaming and hissing. We shook hands with our host.

"Thank you, Mr. Holmes, Dr. Watson. It has been an all too brief association. Perhaps one day you will return to Romania and enjoy a vacation free from the yoke of missions and investigations."

The train whistle gave a shrill blast and we were off on the first leg of our long journey north.

"Well," I said. "Here we go again."

*****

It was much later in the day, when Holmes and I talked once more of our mission and the passage of our enemies. We had travelled without incident between Ploiesti and Buzau and were now rapidly approaching Burcau. Mr. Ionescu had thoughtfully telegraphed ahead to a lady cousin of his who ran a small guesthouse in the town. Although the train was due to arrive after eleven o'clock that evening, she would, nevertheless, be delighted to see us. His cousin's house, he said, was no more than a two minute walk from the station, near to the town clock.

I was still curious about the route taken by the Russians. "Which way are they travelling?" I asked. "As Mr. Ionescu has said, they would hardly have taken the Hungarian or Transylvanian route as the journey would be both unfriendly and onerous. I suppose they could avoid the cities, if as he says Russians are not warmly received in Roumania, but back roads must slow their passage considerably."

"It is a pretty problem, is it not?" said Holmes. "But it is not an insuperable one. I believe that they will use the same logic as when they made their journey from England to Italy, which, my boy, you will recall they made by water."

"As I remember, it was made in order to attract as little attention as possible," I said.

"Quite so," he agreed. "It follows, therefore, that once on the Danube, on the Danube they will stay. In this way they will circumvent Romania and arrive at the more friendly Black Sea port of Odessa."

"Odessa?" I exclaimed.

"Surely that particular course will take them several days," I objected.

"Perhaps, but it is as I have said, they have no inkling of our pursuit and, for as long as they keep within their own timetable, it will not concern them particularly."

"When they arrive at Odessa, what then?"

"It is probable that they will be welcomed by one or more of their confederates. Possibly they may even be relieved of their burden and sent back to England."

"You believe that is possible?" I asked.

"Hunter Andrews is the cargo, and for as long as he is detained, the personnel watching over him may be regarded as unimportant. Indeed, it may be to our particular advantage if Shukin and his associates are relieved, because any replacements may be somewhat less vigilant," he smiled. "There is the additional advantage that Shukin is the only Russian who can positively identify us, but any replacement will not."

Our arrival in Burcau was delayed by more than an hour. Heavy rain in the region had caused the normally well-behaved River Siret to burst its banks and flood the railway line, some ten miles to the south of the town. This was an inconvenience, but there was nothing to be done about it, so Holmes and I chatted idly to a bronzed elderly man who was the only other occupant of our carriage.

"It is always the same," the old man grumbled. "A big downpour and the land around here gets flooded." He pointed to the West. "Although you cannot see them at this time of night, the Moldavian Carpathians collect the rain and send it down here to the valley bottom. Then whoosh, the river, she overflows."

"You seem to know the area very well, sir," I said. "Have you lived here for long?"

"For more than seventy years, young sir," he replied, laughing. "Moldavia is a land over which my kith and kin have travelled for centuries. I am a Zingari, a true Romany. Although of late, I have given up my wanderings, I have become civilised, as the Moldavians say," he laughed again. "But now I am travelling once more on a journey which may be my last."

Much intrigued by the old man, I enquired further about his activities. It transpired that he was on his way to the biggest event in years. The old man, who told us his name was Caroli, was invited to the wedding of Ceran, the 'King of the Gypsies'. Thousands of Romanies were travelling from all over the region to take part in the festivities.

"It will be huge. Gigantic," enthused the old man. "Six days have been set aside, but if the last big wedding is anything to go by; and that was just a cousin from Bessarabia, it will go on for much longer."

Sherlock Holmes was instantly interested. "Is this great event due to take place nearby, sir? We are staying the night in Burcau and time permitting, I would care to witness something of the festivities."

Old Caroli smiled broadly, his yellow teeth peering through the straggling hairs of his whiskers. "If you are in Siret tomorrow, I promise you will see all the gypsies in the world. I am sure you would be welcome."

"Siret," I said. "Is that not the place we stop at before crossing the border?"

"The border?" said the old man sharply. "No one crosses the border these days. At least no Roumanians or foreigners like yourselves. There has been too much friction between the King and the Tsar. They will turn you back for sure."

When eventually we arrived in Barcau, Holmes and I disembarked. Old Caróli remained on board, however, deciding not to break his journey but to travel on to Siret that night. He leaned out of the window. "Try to cross the border if you like, gentlemen. When they turn you back come and look for me. Ask anyone, they all know Caroli. Good Luck!"

Although the midnight hour was close at hand, when eventually we reached our destination, our new host, Miss Popa, proved to be as warm and friendly as her cousin, Mr. Ionescu. It was thanks to the kind ministrations of this spinster lady, that we put the problems of the morrow aside and spent the night deep in the arms of Morpheus.

*****

The morning broke bright and clear. Wrapping the dressing gown around me that had thoughtfully been supplied with the room, I looked out of my window and down on the activities below. In the square hundreds of people were milling about, many were wearing national dress and most were in their Sunday best. All around was cheerful and gay. Then my eye was drawn to the far corner of the square where the church bell began to toll. The doors were thrown open and a procession began. Down the steps came four bearded men dressed entirely in black robes and wearing black birettas; they were Orthodox priests. One was carrying an enormous bible richly tooled in black and gold. Another held a golden crucifix, whilst a third swung about him a smoking thurible. Finally the fourth priest came down the steps holding the figurine of a knight in silver armour. All were chanting and singing. They slowly paraded around the square, gathering a growing army of followers as they walked. Then they ascended the steps of the church once more and disappeared into its darkened interior. An uplifting sight indeed.

"Today is the feast day of St. Stefani, our patron saint," said a voice in my ear, which made me jump. It was Miss Popa, who was carrying a jug of hot water. "Is it not a beautiful sight, Dr. Watson?"

"Indeed, it is," I agreed.

Miss Popa moved swiftly to the bed and began to make it up. Her smooth, economical movements clearly establishing her familiarity with her task. "My cousin Ille tells me you are travelling on an important errand," she remarked.

"That is so," I agreed, as I poured some of the water into the bowl. "Mr. Holmes and I are pursuing some criminals, who have abducted a man from his home in London. If we are correct in our judgement, it will take us to St. Petersburg."

Miss Popa gave the pillow a hearty slap and shook it back into shape. Finally she returned it to the freshly made bed. "Then I have to tell you, Dr. Watson, your mission must fail. You will never be allowed across the border. Ille did not know this when he sent you this way, but the Tsar's troops have recently been stationed near the Ukrainian town of Glybokaya and so far they have turned back anyone who is not Russian who has tried to cross."

Whilst there was no revelation in these words, old Caroli having told us as much the night before, the calm and unfussy way in which she informed me and the certainty in her voice when she told me we would fail, sent a shiver down my spine. Surely we had not travelled all this way only to be thwarted now?

I found Sherlock Holmes at the breakfast table. The problem of the border crossing did not seem to be affecting his appetite. Miss Popa had provided him with a veritable feast. There were eggs, freshly baked bread, butter, honey and coffee. In spite of the possible disappointments the day had in store for us, I decided to assist him in clearing the table as swiftly as maybe. As for the possible problems at the border, Holmes was sanguine.

"Now that we have embarked on this course of action, we have little choice but to see it through. We cannot go across country, Bessarabia is also in Russian hands and we cannot travel there. The only alternative is to turn around and go back the way we have come and travel like our Russian friends to Odessa by sea."

After paying a fond farewell to the excellent Miss Popa, Sherlock Holmes and I recommenced our train journey. For almost five hours we rattled, squealed and bumped our way along the valley bottom. The River Siret was our constant companion, on this stretch. It was a little better-behaved than before. Such flooding as there was confined itself to the lower plains that stretched away towards Bessarabia.

After a packed lunch, Holmes offered me one of his precious and by now, dwindling, supply of cigarettes, which he had brought all the way from London. Feeling the need to stretch his legs, he strolled across the carriage and pulled down the window. For a moment he stood gazing idly at the passing scenery. Then he gave an excited cry. "Watson, my boy. You will really have to take a look at this."

Before us lay what amounted to a small town of multi-coloured tents, wooden caravans, people and horses.

"It is the gypsy wedding," I cried. "We must nearly be in Siret."

It was the gypsy wedding indeed. As we stepped down from the train the sound of music filled our ears. Violins were playing, hands were clapping, voices were singing and laughing and feet were dancing. Indeed, the field by the station was a veritable riot of colour and sounds.

"What a wonderful spectacle," I enthused. "I wonder if we shall be able to find old Caroli?"

Holmes took out his watch. He pulled a face and shook his head. "I am not altogether certain if we will have sufficient time, Watson. According to my timetable, the train from Glybokaya, if we are allowed to board it, leaves in less than one hour. I am afraid that it will take us the best part of that hour to get there."

It was in my heart to tell Holmes that it was possible that any number of trains might be leaving Glybokaya over the next few hours, and it would do no harm if we missed one or two. But common sense prevailed, however, and I meekly collected my haversack from the platform and followed him out into the main street of Siret.

The road to the border proved to be winding and dusty. After a mile or so, Holmes stopped and consulted his guide. "It seems, my dear fellow, that the borders around this particular region do not seem to conform to the rigid demarcations in our part of Europe," he said.

Almost immediately, two military men rode into sight. They threw down their bicycles and advanced upon us. One had a broad Asiatic face. This fellow was no Roumanian. These gentlemen were members of the Tsar's army.

In vain, Holmes tried to make himself understood. He addressed the soldiers in French, English, German and, for the benefit of the Asiatic soldier, Tibetan, a language he had picked up in his sojourn to Lhasa back in 1890s, but all to no avail. The men simply did not comprehend.

Then without warning the European soldier produced a pistol and began waving it at Holmes in a most alarming manner. I took Holmes by the arm and pulled him away; our mission, no matter its importance, was not worth him getting shot.

The impasse was finally resolved by the arrival of a Roumanian policeman, alerted no doubt, by one of the growing number of interested bystanders. Fortunately for us, he spoke passable French and Russian and was able to bring matters to a conclusion. "Now, gentlemen," he said. "It is your desire to leave our country and go into Russia, yes?"

"Indeed," said Holmes.

"Then I have to tell you that your wish cannot be granted. The trooper says no one is allowed into the Ukraine. He also tells me that if you persist he will shoot you."

Realising the futility of further argument, Holmes and I withdrew and trudged the dusty mile back to Siret. Arriving at the station once more, we sat on some tea chests. Feeling completely deflated, I turned to my friend for support and encouragement. "Are we beaten, Holmes? Is this the end of our quest?"

Sherlock Holmes shook his head defiantly. "No, Watson. This is far from the end. As yet I do not know how we shall get into Russia, but get in we shall."

*****

It was perhaps for the best part of an hour that Holmes and I sat in the station yard. Holmes perched like the thinker of old, pipe in mouth, his head swathed in clouds of smoke, mulling over the fate of our mission. In spite of the predicament in which we found ourselves, the heat of the day was causing me to doze off. Suddenly, a rough hand was shaking me. I opened my eyes to see the grinning figure of Caroli standing over me.

"Hello, Doctor. So they sent you back, eh?"

"I'm afraid so," I said gloomily.

Caroli laughed, displaying his yellow teeth. "You should be Zingari; to get across. No one stops us."

Sherlock Holmes jumped to his feet as if galvanised by a thousand volts. "Of course!" he cried. "Watson, I have been slow." He slapped his forehead in self-disgust. "Caroli, we require your assistance. Will you help us?"

The old man nodded. "Of course, Mr. Sherlock, if I can."

"Excellent, then take me please to some of your Northern brethren. I would speak with them."

He jumped down from his perch and shouted to me over his rapidly disappearing shoulder. "Come, Watson! The game is afoot!"

Collecting his discarded haversack, I followed in the wake of Sherlock Holmes. It was through a jostling sea of humanity that Caroli led us, until we stood before a large tent quartered in red and green. The old man called out in Romani to the inhabitants.

"If anyone can help you, it will be Rolo," he said.

A tall, middle-aged woman appeared at the tent flap. Caroli immediately engaged her in conversation.

"Holmes," I said testily. "Why exactly are we traipsing through a gypsy encampment? What is to be gained from it?"

Holmes shook his head and signalled that I should be silent. His reply was both muttered and cryptic. "A moment, my dear fellow. All will be explained shortly."

The woman disappeared under the tent flap once more and we waited in silence for a few moments. Then suddenly the flap was thrown back and a huge black-bearded man in his forties stood there. He smiled at Caroli and shook him warmly by the hand, the force of the handshake almost enough to overbalance the old man. They conversed for several minutes, the eyes of both men falling constantly upon Holmes and myself. Then the face of the gigantic Romani split into a huge grin.

"So, Mr. Sherlock, Mr. Doctor. You desire to become gypsy, eh?"

"Gypsies, we are to become gypsies?" I cried.

"Indeed," said Holmes calmly. "How else would you suppose we may get into Russia?"

Thanks to the valuable assistance of Caroli and the influence of Rolo, Sherlock Holmes was able to arrange safe passage over the border. Fate, in the shape of Rolo's elderly mother, had decreed that he was about to return to his home. Word of her illness had arrived earlier in the day. His wife and children would be left in the care of his cousin, whilst he returned to Hungary to be by her bedside. Holmes and I would accompany him until we reached the town of Chernovtsy. From there we would make our own arrangements.

Rolo invited us into his tent. His wife was to arrange the metamorphosis of Mr. Sherlock and Mr. Doctor into two Romanies. Very soon our travelling clothes had been cast off and replaced by black pantaloons with black boots, dark blue satin shirts and short waistcoats, also black. There was a price to be paid for our new outfits, however. Much of our supplies were appropriated as payment and we were left with only the fresh food and some biscuits. My horn cups, I was thankful to discover, were of no interest. Holmes had earlier joked about turning up at Kiev dressed like Barbary pirates; his prediction it seemed, was about to come true.

It also seemed that the giant Romany was as good as his word about his intention to begin his homeward trek that very evening. Accordingly a cart with two horses between the shafts was brought round. This was a sight that met with my full approval. It had bothered me considerably that we could be once more faced with riding, but any disquiet I had felt about being forced into the saddle had been thankfully dispelled.

It was approaching five in the afternoon when at last we were ready to depart. Rolo had decided to make as much progress as possible before nightfall. He gestured to Holmes and myself that we should take our seats upon the cart. He threw up to me our haversacks, a wineskin and three canvas bags with drawstrings, similar to a sailor's kitbag.

"Here, Mr. Doctor, please hold out your hand," he said. I did as I was bid and felt a soft pasty substance pressed into my palm. I sniffed at it, it smelled quite foul. "Do not worry, it is not poison. Rub it into your skin. Then you will look like me."

Taking my courage into my hands (quite literally) I squeezed the mush between my fingers and rubbed it over my hands and face. Holmes, catching sight of me, began to chuckle. "My dear fellow. Now you begin to resemble a true Romany."

The border was traversed with surprising ease, the Tsar's soldiers scarcely giving us a second glance as we rumbled by. Now I fully understood the simple brilliance of Holmes's plan. Gypsies were regular travellers in this region and little or no notice was taken of them, so they were free to travel with impunity, borders notwithstanding.

Holmes had calculated that Chernovsty would be easily reached by the middle of the next morning. Indeed, half the distance to the town would be covered by nightfall and, if we made an early start, perhaps the Kiev bound train would be waiting for us on our arrival.

Sherlock Holmes and the Bolshevik Plot

After an overnight stop in a small, well-concealed clearing, Sherlock Holmes and I parted company with our travelling companion. Rolo shook us both warmly by the hand and wished us good fortune, whilst we in turn hoped for his mother's full recovery.

The town of Chernovtsy was a two-mile hike from the crossroads where the Romany deposited us. It proved to be a steep and dusty walk, but we arrived in the town without difficulty. One problem facing us, however, was the fact that we were once again strangers in a strange land without a guide to assist us. As in our earlier encounters in Montenegro and Serbia, the Cyrillic alphabet was used, making local signs quite difficult for us to decipher, and there was no Milan to help us.

Despite the difficulties, Holmes managed to purchase the necessary train tickets to Kiev, two of the fifteen roubles given to us by General Wilton as part of our bankroll were spent, but at least we were on our way.

*****

The day had grown considerably colder as our train drew ever nearer to its destination. Spring, so advanced in the Balkans, seemed very late in Ukrainian Russia. A cold gusty wind was blowing as we stepped down onto the platform of the great station at Kiev and I earnestly wished, that I was better dressed against the weather.

I threw down my haversack and gazed at the sea of people surrounding us. Quite close by there stood a number of gaily-dressed men, their yellow, deeply-lined faces wreathed with smiles. Beyond stood a crowd of dusty, sunburned individuals, some carrying large sacks on their backs and most with large stout staves in their hands. Turning around to gaze upon more of these wondrous sights, I almost fell into two swarthy black-bearded men, dressed entirely in black and wearing tall hats with large furry brims.

Sherlock Holmes took my arm and pulled me back. "We appear to be standing in the middle of the world's crossroads, Doctor," he remarked.

"Indeed, or we have been accidentally deposited into the midst of a three-ringed circus."

"La cirque magnifique," said Holmes, laughing.

Suddenly, a small dark man with a pronounced limp detached himself from the crowd. He tugged Holmes by the sleeve and addressed him in French. "Ah, Monsieur, you are French perhaps?"

"No, sir. We are English, but we both speak French."

"That is excellent. Permit me to introduce myself. I am Henri Rougier. I am the driver and the general factotum of the brothers of the Monastery of the Cave. Perhaps you wish me to take you there?"

Sherlock Holmes looked him up and down. "We have come to Kiev to speak with the Patriarch. If you desire to assist us then you may take my companion and myself to his residence."

The little man looked at us for a moment, then he shrugged his shoulders. "The Patriarch is presently to be found at the Monastery of St Michael of the Golden Domes, but one destination is as good as another," he grinned at us, displaying crooked teeth. "I will take you there." He briskly rubbed his hands together. "If you will wait by the main entrance, I shall bring the car for you."

As the strange little man disappeared into the throng, I expressed my doubts about him to Holmes. "Are we to trust the fellow?" I asked. "After all, here we are strangers in a strange land. We may have allowed ourselves to fall into the hands of an unscrupulous villain, set upon robbing, or indeed, delivering us into the clutches of others who are willing to rob us."

Holmes shook his head.

"No, Doctor. This fellow is no villain bent on depriving us of our worldly goods." He grasped the hem of his short black jacket and held it up for my inspection. "I cannot but think even if Monsieur Rougier has designs on the valuables of travellers, he would waste his energies on two Englishmen dressed as gypsies."

I surveyed my clothing and nodded in agreement.

"Indeed," Holmes chuckled. "He may possibly be inclined to pity us and treat us with more consideration than we deserve."

We picked up our haversacks and walked to the appointed spot at the main entrance of the station. A few moments later a large black motor car drew up and the sharp features of the little Frenchman peered out at us. "Here we are, gentlemen. Please get in."

Holmes threw our haversacks in beside the driver, whilst I sank into the soft leather seat at the rear. The car roared into life and we were off down the long wide concourse leading to the main route to the city centre. Looking through the rear window, I could see the station in its entirety. There was a tall three-storied central block, through which we had just passed, and two huge wings, each running some two hundred feet in length. The whole edifice (to my untutored eye, I have to admit), resembled nothing less than a mid nineteenth century country house, built on a gigantic scale. This with a railway running through it.

Holmes sniffed the air. "The city has a particular odorous quality about it. Do you not think so, Watson?" he remarked.

Holmes was exactly right. From the very moment I had stepped down from the train I had been aware of a particular sweet, yet burning smell filling my nostrils. It was an aroma I seemed to recognise, yet it was one that I was unable to readily identify. In many ways it resembled the smell of seaside candyfloss, the delight of so many day-trippers, but here in Kiev?

Monsieur Rougier briefly looked over his shoulder. He nodded and smiled. "Ah, you must be referring to the smell from the sugar refineries, Monsieur. There are many on the outskirts of the city." He pointed to the right of the road, where the land fell away down a steep hill. "There, in the Demieska, you will see the chimneys of Brodsky's refinery, which is the largest. It employs many Kievans." He chuckled. "It also makes Mr. Brodsky very rich."

It was then I saw to our left a large white building set in its own parkland. It was raised in the Palladian style and if it had been dropped down suddenly into the Sussex countryside, it would not have looked out of place. "What a magnificent construction," I murmured.

"Indeed," said Holmes. "A Vanburgh or a Hawksmoor would have been hard pressed to produce a more impressive sight."

The motor car stopped abruptly. Our driver had braked very hard to avoid three young men in the roadway, who were apparently entirely oblivious to our presence. "Students," he cried in exasperated tones. "Their heads are too full of books and too empty of the nature of this world."

The little Frenchman slowly engaged first gear and we pulled away again, moving carefully in an effort to avoid the perfect scrum of young men milling about in the roadway. "This is the University of St. Vladimir," he announced. "It is named after the First Christian ruler of Kiev. Once the university was said to be one of the world's great seats of learning, although in latter years its luminescence has faded somewhat."

Looking around, I smiled at Holmes. "Then I would have dearly desired to count the student numbers at the height of the university's popularity."

"Are you gentlemen accommodated?" our driver queried. "If you are not, I can recommend to you the National Hotel in the Kreschatik. We are about to turn into the street and I shall indicate it to you when we pass it by."

"Do you suppose that two irregularly dressed fellows such as ourselves would be welcomed in an elegant establishment like the National, Monsieur Rougier?" Holmes asked.

"Oh, when I explain to them that their guests are none other than the celebrated detective, Sherlock Holmes, and his friend and associate Dr. Watson, I have no doubt that the management will be pleased to welcome you with open arms."

Holmes chuckled. "Excellent, sir. You have found us out. Why, I believe it is you and not I who is the detective."

"How did you discover us?" I asked.

Monsieur Rougier laughed again. "When two Englishmen arrive on a train from the middle of nowhere and ask to be taken to see the Patriarch of Kiev, a certain question arises in my mind. Who are they? When they speak excellent French, unlike so many of their compatriots, it occurs to me that they are gentlemen. This is borne out, not by their dress, however, but by the formal way in which they address each other. When earlier, you smoked a cigarette, Mr. Holmes, I could not help but notice the monogram "S.H." on the case. Then, when your travelling companion called you "Holmes", it seemed to me that 'S. Holmes' could only be Sherlock Holmes. Knowing you to be intimate with only one other person, Dr. John Watson, I concluded that it was entirely possible that you were Holmes and Watson."

He paused for a long moment, as if waiting to let the matter sink in. "And beside," he continued coolly. "Your photographs were heavily featured in Kiev's main newspaper, *Rada*, some months ago when rumours of your supposed return from retirement were circulating Europe."

Sherlock Holmes slapped his leg and laughed loudly. "My dear, Rougier. You are quite inestimable. The brothers of the Monastery of the Cave are indeed fortunate to have you in their employ."

As the motor car was turned into the Kreshchatik a sight met my eyes which caused some considerable surprise. The street was simply littered with other vehicles. Many were horse-drawn, some were steam driven and electric tramcars travelled their rails. The well-populated street had many shop signs in French, Russian and Ukrainian and there were electric street lamps!

"Good heavens," I cried. "This could almost be Oxford Street."

As we rode along the Kreshchatik, Monsieur Rougier pointed out many of the sights. "Kiev is an international city," he said. "Look about you and you will see people from all over the known world ... Over there," he said, pointing to a large stone building. "The City Hall. There by the statue of the Archangel Michael. Those bearded men, they are Turks selling little sweet cakes called Hala. Over by that corner are some Chinese selling silks."

"Indeed," said Holmes. "There were some of their fellows at the station when we arrived."

"You also must have seen the pilgrims, 'God's Workers' as they are known, waiting by the exit. They come from Bessarabia, Austria, Bohemia, Perm, Irkustsk, even Astrakhan. They come to the Monastery of the Cave. But they do not ride as you do, it is their mission to walk all the way, so walk they do."

Rougier turned the motor car left and we drove up a steep incline which would take us to the old city. He pointed out a large statue standing proudly upon the hilltop as that of St. Vladimir, the founder of Kiev. Looking across the valley I could see a dark, slow moving river.

"That is the Dnepro," said the Frenchman. "You will see the port below, where much of the city's produce is exported and its needs are imported. It is unfortunate, though, that too much of the city's effluence and a good deal of other waste is allowed to foul the river. In my fifteen years, the mess has become progressively worse."

As our vehicle breasted the rise, I was once more aware of many people in the large plaza before us. Ordinary Russians dressed in peasant's clothing. Holmes enquired of our driver the reason for this particular congregation. He replied, "They are waiting for the Patriarch. He must be returning to St. Sophia and his residence."

"Why are they waiting for the Patriarch?" I asked.

"They come here with letters of appeal, begging for his help in matters both spiritual and temporal." He pulled on the handbrake and the motor car ground to a halt. "There is the Patriarch," he cried. "This is not good news for you, sirs. When the letters are received he will shut himself away for many days so he may pray for the succour of those who are in need, and will not see anyone."

"What shall we do, Holmes?" I asked. "Time is one commodity of which we are in short supply. We cannot simply hang around for days, until the Patriarch will see us, but without his assistance we can never hope to gain an audience with the Tsar."

Suddenly, Holmes threw open the door and sprinted towards the crowd. The Patriarchs cortège had walked across the square and was now almost level with the faithful and there was much cheering and shouting. Now I could see him clearly. He was a tall robust man in his sixties, with a long grey beard. On his head he wore a mitre of black and silver and his robes, also of silver, hung in great folds to his feet.

As the pontiff moved on his stately passage, many hands were thrust at him, all containing notes or letters in them. Then I saw Sherlock Holmes leaping into the throng and physically forcing himself to the front. Then it was his hand that was thrust to the fore. In a flash I realised his motive. The letter from Father Grigory at the Monastir Moraca in Montenegro was in his grasp.

Then I saw one of the entourage take the letter. He looked at it briefly, then handed it to another. They appeared to hold a short conversation, then the second man ran over to one of the priests immediately to the rear of the Patriarch. He too looked at the letter and even from the distance I was sitting, I could see clearly the look of surprise on the cleric's face.

Stepping out of line he looked back into the crowd for the bearer of the letter. The first man who had taken it from Holmes's out stretched hand, pointed him out and they quickly advanced upon my friend. I tapped Monsieur Rougier on the shoulder. "Holmes has succeeded in getting attention, start up the car, my dear fellow, we may need to get to him quickly."

Once more the engine roared into life and we slowly bumped our way over the cobbled surface of the plaza. Holmes, by now had moved away from the crowd and was sitting on the plinth of a large statue talking to the priest who had sought him out.

"Ah, Watson," he cried as I jumped out of the car. "This is excellent. Father Michael here has recognised the insignia of the Monastir Moraca and wishes to know how we came by this letter. I have told him something of our task and he has promised that he will do everything in his power to arrange an audience with the Patriarch."

"Can the priest say when we may see the Patriarch?" I enquired.

"He says that the pontiff has a little time set aside tonight after evensong and may see us then. But we should be prepared for a disappointment, because he may wish to rest."

Monsieur Rougier, ever attentive to our needs, agreed to take us back to the Kreshchatik and install us in the National Hotel. There we would wash and change into clothing more suitable for a formal meeting with the Patriarch. If we were sent for, he would collect us and take us to St. Sophia.

It was a little after four when Holmes and I sat down together for a well-deserved drink and smoke. We had decided on two new suits of late nineteenth century design, at least. In the more fashionable areas of London or Paris, the clothes would have seemed outdated. But Monsieur Rougier assured us that we were dressed in the highest of fashion for Kiev. Holmes was sanguine about our apparel, however. "Well, Watson. In spite of your worst fears and my best efforts we will not meet the Patriarch dressed like Barbary pirates after all."

He stood up and walked over to the window where he stood for a few moments surveying the rapidly growing afternoon gloom. "My dear fellow," he suddenly said. "It is starting to snow."

I stood up also and followed Holmes to the window.

"Indeed," I said. "The temperature has fallen considerably since this morning, so I cannot say that I am entirely surprised."

One of the hotel staff appeared at my elbow. He did not speak, but merely bowed as he held out a silver salver with an envelope upon it.

"This must be a communication from the Patriarch," I said eagerly, holding the envelope up for Holmes's inspection.

Holmes reached out and took the letter from me. He looked at it briefly, then shook his head. "No, my dear fellow, this letter is not from the Patriarch."

"It is not?" I cried. "Then from whom has it come? Surely no one else knows of our presence in Kiev."

"Apart from the obvious fact that the writer of this epistle is a woman well past middle age, that she is extremely wealthy, well informed and influential, I cannot see that there is much to deduce." He handed the envelope back to me. "Here, Watson, see for yourself."

"My dear Holmes," I said laughing. "How do you deduce that the sender is a lady?"

"Tsk. The perfume."

"That she is of extreme wealth?"

"The heavy cream cartridge paper from which the envelope has been produced. A guinea a packet, or I am no judge."

"She is well informed?"

"She knew that we are here."

"She is influential?"

"Who else but a women of influence would be able to send a note to two patrons of an International Hotel with the expectation of it being delivered without demur?"

"Indeed. But what about the lady being well past middle age?"

"Look at the handwriting, my boy. It rather resembles the effort that a spider might make, had it fallen into the inkwell, then crawled across the envelope. Only an elderly hand would produce such a script."

"It could have been written by an elderly retainer to a young woman."

"Who would keep in their employ a secretary whose hand was so unsteady? No, it is the script of the lady herself."

I took out my penknife and slit the envelope. Inside was an equally expensive sheet of cream paper. "Look at this, Holmes," I said. "The letter is from a lady, Madam Julia Veselitska." Here Holmes raised an eyebrow. "She welcomes us to Kiev and hopes that we are well and enjoying our visit to the city. If time permits, she would greatly appreciate our attendance at a soirée she is giving tomorrow night – R S V P."

"Well now, Doctor. Our fame precedes us," Holmes chuckled.

"But how could the lady know of our presence?"

"Influence … and perhaps a little bird has been singing."

"Rougier," I cried.

"Dr. Watson," said a voice I knew well. "You are calling me?" It was none other than the little Frenchman in person.

Holmes adopted a stern face. "Monsieur Rougier, what is the meaning of this letter?"

Rougier almost jumped into the air, his eyes wide with surprise and alarm as he espied the note. "She has written to you already?" he spluttered. "I have just come from her office. I had no idea she would communicate with you so swiftly."

Following the lead set by Sherlock Holmes, I looked sharply at him. "Sir, this is a gross infringement of our privacy."

Monsieur Rougier was almost crushing his hat in his embarrassed hands. "I am so sorry, gentlemen. It was not my intention to have this happen. Please let me explain; it is one of my little enterprises. Whenever any new and interesting people arrive in Kiev, I inform Madam of their arrival. If she deems these people to be worthy of her company she will invite them to one of her social events, then she pays me four roubles for the information, if the visitor is a worthy one."

Holmes looked sharply at the little Frenchman. "Now let me see. You work for the Brothers of the Monastery of the Cave. At the same time you are running your own private motor cab service. You also act as an agent for the National Hotel and for Madam Veselitska. I have no doubt you are acting for the tailor from whom you obtained our clothes."

"Indeed, sir," Rougier agreed. "But the tailor is a countryman of mine. It seems right and proper for me to promote his business."

Holmes relaxed into a smile. "I have said it before, Monsieur Rougier. You are a resourceful man."

Rougier relaxed visibly and smiled also. "It is hard work and time consuming, but I believe it is better than a job at Brodskys," he said.

Holmes's interest in the matter was not satiated, however. "Perhaps you will tell us something about this Madam Veselitska," he said.

"She is the pivot upon which Kievian high society turns, Mr. Holmes," he replied. "I believe that she is Polish by birth. At any rate, she is the widow of Russia's last envoy to the Great Khan of the Crimea, when the Turks ruled there. When anyone who is anyone arrives in Kiev, they will be quickly brought into her elevated circle."

"Well now, Rougier. This is one occasion when Madam Veselitska must be disappointed. Please inform the good lady that unfortunately Dr. Watson and I will be unable to attend her soirée. We are intending to spend just twenty-four hours in Kiev. Please convey our apologies."

Rougier nodded his assent. "Of course, Mr. Holmes."

"Well now, Monsieur Rougier," I said taking to my chair once more. "Have you sought us out for the pleasure of our company, or was there something in particular you wanted to say to us?"

The little Frenchman's face suddenly became a living mask of horror and consternation. Several times he slapped his face quite hard. "My dear sirs. I had quite forgotten the message I carry for you. The Patriarch desires you to attend him this evening. He would also like you to join him for supper. I am so sorry. Talk of Madame's letter quite put the matter out of my mind."

"At what o'clock does the Patriarch desire our company."

"At seven ... in two hours."

"Never mind, my dear fellow," said Holmes. "At least we have obtained our heart's desire. Come Watson," he cried. "The Patriarch awaits us."

Five

Patriarch Alexi showed Holmes and myself to fireside chairs. His room was quite small and was hung with gorgeous tapestries. Although it was still quite early in the day the dusk was rapidly arriving. The Patriarch spoke in Russian to his servant who attacked the fire until there was a bright blaze in the hearth. Then the young man bowed low and silently made his exit.

"I hope you are warm enough gentlemen?" said our host in French. "I have sent Feyodor to make tea. I hope you like Russian tea."

The Patriarch sat back in his chair and eyed Holmes and myself quizzically. Clearly our western garb was new to him. "You have travelled to Kiev by way of the Balkans," he said. "That must have been a tortuous journey."

"Indeed," said Holmes. "We have driven over many long and uneven paths."

Patriarch Alexi laughed. "Unlike your English roads, Mr. Holmes." He stroked his generous beard thoughtfully. "What did you make of that backward region?"

Holmes glanced in my direction. "On the way, Milan, our guide, told us something of the history of the Balkans. We found it of considerable interest."

"A sad and cruel history," said the Patriarch.

"Does Russia have such a tale to tell?" I asked.

"Indeed, much blood has been spilled during the forging of the Russian empire, too much of it by our own people."

Our tea was interrupted by a heavy knock at the door and the appearance of the angular form of the Patriarch's servant. He bowed towards Holmes and myself, then spoke quietly with his master. The Patriarch nodded and gestured to his servant who turned on his heels and silently withdrew once more.

The Patriarch stood up. "Father Paul, the Prelate of Smolensk, is here. Coomeen fazzer," he said in English.

A tall sallow-faced young man entered the room. He was dressed entirely in black. A gold crucifix hung from a chain around his waist. He took off the black biretta he was wearing and bowed low.

"Good efternoon, fazzer Paul," said the Patriarch in English. "Dis ees Meester 'Olmes and Docter Watsin."

"Good day, gentlemen," said the young man in perfect English. "I am glad to meet you. I have heard so much about your adventures, but I never thought to actually meet you one day."

Holmes and I rose to greet our visitor.

"Hello father," I said, offering my hand. "May I compliment you on the standard of your English."

Father Paul laughed. "It is not such a remarkable feat, Dr. Watson. I was born and brought up in Southampton and spent the first dozen or so years of my life almost exclusively speaking English."

Patriarch Alexi said, in French, "Father Paul knows the reason for your coming here. He will go with you to St. Petersburg."

*****

The St. Petersburg bound train rattled and bumped along many a weary mile. Kiev had become little more than a distant memory and our eyes now fell upon acres of scrub, much of it marshy.

Now, it is an indisputable fact that long train journeys tend to become wearisome, because there is so very little to do except sit, stand, lie down, talk, eat, or sleep. For some six hours, I had done all of these things to a greater or a lesser extent, and to be quite frank, had become bored to tears. The French novel I had purchased upon departure was appallingly silly and turgid and I had perceived the identity of the villain before a quarter of the book had been read.

I gazed idly at my companions. Sherlock Holmes had composed himself in a corner seat and had apparently ascended to a higher plane of mental activity, a habit he had earlier assured me that was better for him, in every way than the pernicious seven per cent solution of cocaine, in which he had indulged himself earlier in our association.

Father Paul on the other hand, was quite genuinely asleep. Latterly he had produced his bible, but on this particular journey there existed more spare hours than even the most dedicated biblical scholar could expect to fill in his pursuit of the word.

I stood up and quietly walked across the gently rocking carriage. Pulling down the window, I gazed at the flat featureless plain. Coarse scrubby grass was growing in abundance, but few trees, save the twisted and stunted variety, were to be seen. As I watched, a black smudge in the distance slowly became the buildings of a small town, perhaps some ten miles away as yet. Then at last, I espied several trees protected, no doubt, from the harsh environment by the buildings that surrounded them. I wondered as the town slowly moved nearer, if the train would stop, or as before, it would continue on its steady procession and ignore the opportunity.

Further down the train, towards the guard's van, another passenger had probably become bored with his companions and, like myself, had taken the opportunity to view the scenery.

For a moment I could only see the back of his blond head, then he turned to face my direction. I prepared my smile of greeting and raised my hand for a genial wave, but as his face came into sight, my smile became frozen into a grimace and my hand clenched into a fist. It was Shukin.

I looked again. Shukin it was. The cruel handsome face of the Russian had forever been burned into my mind's eye. It was as if the events of that terrible night in Sussex when Holmes and I had faced him and his ill fated companion at gun point had occurred just twenty-four hours ago.

The Russian clearly saw the startled look on my face. He appeared initially to be puzzled by my reaction, then I saw his eyes widen as he recognised me also and I knew instantly that the lives of my companions and myself were in the gravest danger. The followers of Ulyanov were, without doubt, desperate men, who would stop at nothing to achieve their ends and they would not baulk at killing anyone who stood in their way.

I felt in my pocket for my service revolver and smiled grimly to myself, the comforting bulge was still there. Quickly I felt into my inside jacket pocket and retrieved the clip of bullets. I made a swift mental calculation, nine, no ten bullets remained after the incident on the river Jura, when I was forced to fire upon the minions of Bogachavich.

I turned to my companions, who remained, as yet, blissfully unaware of their mortal danger. "Holmes, Father Paul," I cried, shaking them rather roughly in my haste.

Without awaiting their acknowledgement, I swiftly moved to the end of the carriage nearest to that of the guard's van, where the door stood ajar. I wondered if it was possible to lock it. It was a flimsy structure, but would provide a temporary barrier for our enemies. I shut the door with a bang, but to my dismay there seemed to be no visible means of locking it.

"A wedge, I need a wedge," I muttered. "It may delay them for a while."

"My dear fellow," said Sherlock Holmes from right behind me. "Why on earth do you require a wedge?"

I explained the situation. "It is a good idea, Watson," he said calmly. "But even if we locked, bolted and chained this door, it is so insubstantial, it would not withstand even the first blow."

"Then what are we to do?"

The penetrating glance of Sherlock Holmes ran swiftly around the carriage. "When they come, they will expect us to be sheltering from them and have taken refuge at the far end of the carriage, but you and I, Watson will have secreted ourselves on the floor under these first row of seats." He called out to the priest. "Father Paul, please gather up our luggage and heap it up on the seat at the end of the carriage. Then, if you value your safety, I advise you to conceal yourself."

The priest nodded and obeyed Holmes's advice without demur. He quickly piled the bags up on the seat and stood there only half concealed. "There you are, Mr. Holmes. The perfect rat in a trap."

From the other side of the door, I detected the sounds of movement. Holmes signalled for Father Paul to hide. "Now, Watson," he said quietly. "There is just sufficient room for us to squeeze ourselves under the seats." The door handle began to turn slowly. "Quickly, my dear fellow, they are almost upon us."

From the prone position I could see only the bottom of the door as it slowly opened. There came a sharp click, which I recognised as the sound of a pistol being cocked. Suddenly the door was thrown back against the partitioning wall with a bang and two pairs of black-booted feet appeared in my line of sight.

There came a shouted order from one of the newcomers, then I heard the quiet voice of Father Paul. From the lips of our enemies, came the names of Holmes and Watson. The priest spoke again, and by the tone of his voice I could tell that he was professing his ignorance of us; and by the anger in the voice of the Russians, that they patently did not believe him.

Cautiously, I drew my revolver and looked over at Holmes who also had his gun ready. Holmes held up a hand and signalled for me to follow his lead. Slowly and cautiously he rolled out of his hiding place. Standing up quickly and silently he pointed his pistol at our enemies. "Shukin," he said sharply. "Please put up your hands."

The Russian spun on his heel and looked at Holmes with blank amazement upon his face. His companion, however, was much more ready for action. He pulled his gun and fired it immediately. The bullet whizzed past the head of Sherlock Holmes who ducked instantly. Shukin, who by now had regained his composure somewhat, became galvanised into action. Firing his gun in my direction, he threw himself through the doorway by which he had entered the carriage. There came a searing pain from my right hand and I dropped my revolver. In the next moment Shukin's companion made to follow his friend, but was felled by a sharp blow to the neck by the hand of Father Paul, who kicked the carriage door shut in the same instant.

Holmes gazed at my bleeding hand with worried eyes. "Watson, my boy. Are you much hurt?" he exclaimed.

"No," I replied. "It is nothing, merely a flesh wound." I pulled out my handkerchief and wound it around my hand. "There we are, it is as good as new."

Father Paul hauled the unconscious Russian onto one of the seats. He smiled. "Unfortunately our plans seem to have been only partly successful," he remarked.

Sherlock Holmes looked at the priest with undisguised surprise and no little respect. "My dear Father Paul, you are full of surprises."

The priest laughed. "It is an example of a misspent youth, Mr. Holmes."

Suddenly, the door at the farthest end of the carriage burst open and a large red-faced man with short-cropped hair and a generous moustache stood there. He snapped out what appeared to be an angry series of questions. Father Paul answered him and there followed a brief conversation in Russian.

"Who is this fellow?" I asked the priest.

"He is Mr Michailichenko, a senior Okhrana man, the Tsar's secret police. He is demanding to know who is discharging firearms."

Sherlock Holmes surveyed the policeman for a brief moment. "You had better explain our situation, Father Paul, as it would be as well to have an officer of the law on our side."

Once more, the priest and the policeman conversed in Russian. Then the Okhrana man addressed Holmes and myself in bad French. "You are Mr. Holmes and Dr. Watson?"

"We are," Holmes agreed.

"And you are pursuing the men of Ulyanov?"

"Indeed."

"Then we are on the same side. These bad men have been in my sight since Kiev, when I was informed they were on the train from Odessa." At this point Holmes looked at me knowingly. "We shall help each other now."

"Quite so," agreed Holmes.

Mr. Michailichenko frowned. "Your friend, Mr. Andrews, he is in danger now they are discovered."

Sparing us little time to digest this crumb of comfort, the policeman took out a whistle and blew it. Almost immediately three large uniformed men carrying rifles appeared in the doorway. Mr. Michailichenko waved them on down the carriage and signalled that we should follow on.

As we travelled through the train, one thing became abundantly clear, there were very few other passengers. I remarked on the matter to Father Paul and his reply surprised me greatly. "It is no mystery, Dr. Watson. The railway system in Russia is not run for the benefit of her people, most could scarcely afford the fares. No, it runs for the advantage of the nobility, the officials of the state and other well-to-do people. If the train has paying passengers, all well and good. If not, at least it is keeping the rust off the rails for the benefit of the Royal train, for it would not do to have rusty rails when the Tsar takes his annual holiday in the Crimea."

Suddenly I was thrown forward into Father Paul, as the train lurched to a grinding halt. All, including Sherlock Holmes, were thrown heavily to the floor. Attempting to disengage myself from the arms and legs of my companions, I wondered what had happened.

"Someone has thrown the emergency brake in the baggage car," cried Mr. Michailichenko.

"It must be the Russians," I spluttered, quite forgetting the obvious fact that almost everyone on the train was Russian.

Holmes scrambled to his feet and looked through the external carriage door. Throwing it open, he half jumped, half fell onto the track below.

"Holmes?" I cried, alarmed at his sudden disappearance.

"Watson," came his reply. "Get me a rifle, hurry, man!"

Turning to the policeman nearest to me, I snatched the weapon from his surprised grasp, and threw it down to my companion.

Then I saw what Holmes had seen. Several figures were scrambling up the railway embankment. Clearly, they were intent on escaping to the little town ahead. One, however, was lagging behind his companions, hampered by the man he was almost dragging along behind him. The man was, without doubt, Hunter Andrews.

Slowly and methodically, Sherlock Holmes raised the rifle to his shoulder. Suddenly I realised his intention to shoot the Russian. "Be careful, Holmes," I murmured.

Sherlock Holmes chuckled, but there was no humour in his voice. "I am always careful, Doctor," he said evenly.

Gently Holmes squeezed the trigger and the rifle burst into life; in spite of my foreknowledge of the event, I was startled by it. Then, the man, as if he had been punched by an invisible hand, was knocked spinning to the ground. Before I could move a muscle, Holmes was running across the track bed and scrambling up the embankment towards the fallen Russian and his struggling captive.

The Okhrana men jumped down from the carriage, the one I had relieved of his weapon giving me a particularly unfriendly look, and set off in pursuit of Holmes. Then, from somewhere hidden in the small copse of stunted trees above the embankment, there came the sound of rapid gunfire. The surviving Russians were now firing upon us! Several bullets whizzed past my head before embedding themselves in the woodwork behind me and I threw myself to the floor, a part of the train with which I felt myself becoming intimately acquainted.

It was at this point that the Okhrana men decided to return fire on the men in the trees and for several terrible moments, I thought myself to be in a scene from one of those wild west films so popular at the time with schoolboys.

Then, just as suddenly, the firing ceased and all was silent and pacific.

"Watson!" It was the voice of Holmes. "Give a hand, old fellow."

I scrambled to the door and peered out. "I am here, are you safe?"

"Quite safe and well, but I am concerned for our friend Mr. Andrews. When his captor fell back down the embankment, I am afraid that he was taken with him and as a consequence has had a nasty knock."

I reached down and seized the dazed young man by the shoulders and with the help of my friend managed to get him into the carriage.

"Come along, Holmes," I cried as I helped my friend aboard. "The shooting has stopped but there may still be considerable danger."

Holmes stepped into the carriage. He smiled grimly. "I think not, Doctor. The police are at this very moment rounding up our adversaries."

"And the fellow you brought down?"

Holmes shook his head. "Unfortunately, he is dead, the fall broke his neck. It is a bitter irony, Watson, because the wound I inflicted upon him was sufficient only to injure him slightly."

"I am sorry to hear that," I said. "All human life, no matter how low, is of value." I patted Holmes on the shoulder. "But these things happen."

A groan from Hunter Andrews was sufficient to put the matter out of my mind. For any doctor the needs of the living outweigh the concerns for the dead, and John H. Watson, M.D. is no exception. A brief examination of the young man found him to be rather less damaged than first appearances would have implied. Certainly, he was very much bruised and somewhat battered, but he was only very slightly concussed.

"Oh, my head," he moaned, looking quizzically at me with those dark gypsy eyes, so well described by his excellent wife. "I feel as if I have been run over by an omnibus. Where in the world am I?"

"You are safe and free of your captors," I told him.

He sat up and rubbed his head. "Could I have a little water, please?"

Sherlock Holmes brought the young man some water in one of my horn cups. Andrews took a drink and attempted to rise to his feet.

"Where am I?" he said again. "And who are you gentlemen?"

Holmes helped the unsteady man to one of the seats. He sat down opposite. "I am Sherlock Holmes, and this is my friend and colleague, Dr. Watson. We are presently on board a train bound for St. Petersburg and we have travelled a long and weary mile to meet here today."

The next few moments were taken up by Holmes's explanation of the train of events which had led to this meeting. Hunter Andrews, it transpired, had no notion about how far he had travelled and how distant he had become removed from hearth and home.

"The last thing I can clearly remember, Mr. Holmes, is the suite of offices in London, where the Russians held me for several days. I do not know just for how long I have been away from home."

I looked at the young man's travel worn clothes and his battered and filthy condition and sadly shook my head. Taking out my notebook, I examined the notes I had made.

"Today is the thirty-first of March, you were abducted on the third of March. That was some twenty-eight days ago," I said.

Andrews shook his head. "Indeed? I had no idea."

There came the sound of activity from the track-side and the head of Mr. Michailichenko appeared. He was rather red faced and dusty. Then the first of his captives was abruptly and roughly thrust through the opening. It was Shukin. His blonde hair was much disarranged and his clothes were filthy and torn. Then came a clanking sound and the manacles that held him were thrown into the carriage by an Okhrana man. Shukin glared at the assembly, but appeared to be too exhausted to speak. He was swiftly followed by the policeman, from whom I had earlier taken the rifle, then by the surviving kidnappers and the Okhrana men who had captured them.

At a signal from Mr. Michailichenko they were dragged away without ceremony to spend the remainder of the long journey securely shackled and guarded by the Okhrana men, until the Tsar's courts could deal with them in St. Petersburg.

*****

It was later that afternoon when our company settled down once more. Hunter Andrews had by now recovered and was looking clean and tidy once more. His old clothes had been discarded and with the help of Father Paul and myself, from whom he had borrowed a clean shirt, trousers and a pullover, he was almost a new man.

Mr. Michailichenko was in an expansive mood and it gave him considerable amusement to hear about our trek across the wilder parts of Europe, chasing these Bolsheviks as he called them. From his waistcoat pocket, he took out a silver flask and offered it around. Father Paul shook his head, but Holmes, Andrews and myself accepted the offer.

The clear colourless liquid reminded me rather of gin, but the taste most certainly did not. Indeed, I rather spluttered and coughed over my first mouthful of this fiery liquid. The policeman laughed. "Do you like it, Dr. Watson?"

"Very much," I agreed. "But what is it?"

"It is Vodka. Russia's national drink."

"It is certainly very fortifying," said I, wiping my eyes.

Hunter Andrews had said little about his experiences, but the matter was evidently playing on his mind. "Mr. Holmes, now you have rescued me and brought my captors to justice, so to speak, your mission must surely be over?"

Sherlock Holmes shook his head. "Not, quite, Mr. Andrews. We may have succeeded, but we still need to uncover their motive, or how it may affect the safety of the Tsar."

"Then you believe that there is more to discover?"

"Indeed. Ulyanov had you kidnapped because of your specialist knowledge and to do a specific job. It is something to do with safes, strong rooms or some other place for which there is no key."

Mr. Michailichenko grunted. "You are exactly right, Mr. Holmes. The motive is as yet unclear, but we in the Okhrana have methods available, which will loosen even the most stubborn tongue. When we reach St. Petersburg, there will be no need for you to tarry, Mr. Holmes. The Tsar will be protected by my men."

Holmes looked expressively in my direction, but did not comment. Police arrogance was no new experience, neither apparently, was it confined to the denizens of Scotland Yard.

It was only later, when Holmes and I were alone, that he opened his mind to me. Midnight had come and gone and we were enjoying a last pipe before bed. By this late hour, ours were the only lamps burning in the carriage, perhaps the entire train. Indeed the only other souls I imagined to be awake were the engine driver and his mate.

Holmes sat cross-legged on the seat opposite blowing smoke rings and looking somewhat pensive. "We were very fortunate today, Watson," he said at last. "Our enemies allowed themselves to fall into our laps."

"Very possibly," said I. "But good fortune, like a motorcycle, has to be kick-started. Did you not predict the exact movements of those fellows? Indeed could it not be said that in some ways, this was a trap into which they fell?"

Holmes frowned. "You are very kind, old fellow, and possibly you may be right, but it is as I have remarked, their capture does not bring with it the vital information we need."

"You cannot hazard a guess?" I asked.

"Watson, you know that I do not guess. It is a shocking habit which leads to unsatisfactory results."

"Then do you have a theory?" I persisted.

He sighed. "So far I have constructed four scenarios, each more disquieting than its predecessor, without data I cannot speculate, however."

I sighed. "Well, perhaps a good night's sleep will assist your mental processes," I said.

"Sleep!" he said sharply. "That is the farthest thing from my mind. No, Watson, you take to your bunk and rest. I will stay up for a little while," he chuckled. "If I had tobacco, I would be informing you that this was quite a three pipe problem. As we have just consumed the last of our supply, however, I shall be forced to think unaided and unfortified."

Six

I had enjoyed a thoroughly pleasant day. Sherlock Holmes had solved a particularly baffling case and the supplier of the vital clue to the identity of the miscreant was none other than John H. Watson, M.D.

A smiling Holmes had clapped me on the back and declared me to be the most excellent of fellows. Later he sat me down before one of Mrs. Hudson's most toothsome steak and kidney pies. Then, placing me in his favourite chair, with the horsehair stuffing falling out of it, he eulogised on my foresight and perspicacity.

Mrs. Hudson appeared by my elbow and placed a tray of drinks on the table. "Well done, Dr. Watson," she said as she laid her hand on my shoulder and squeezed it. "Well done indeed."

But something was wrong. Mrs. Hudson was squeezing my shoulder too hard, much too hard. This was certainly no way for a landlady to be treating a paying lodger. In vain I tried to remonstrate with the lady, but the words would not come and all the time she was shaking me.

"Watson, Watson." The voice of Sherlock Holmes was calling me now. Then I opened my eyes and it was he who was standing over me. "Hello, old man," he said gently. "We have almost reached our destination. Father Paul says we shall be in St. Petersburg in fifteen minutes."

I yawned and stretched. I had been dreaming. My back and shoulders were stiff from the unaccustomed position they had adopted during my nap. I shivered, the temperature in the carriage had fallen considerably as we had travelled North. Looking idly through the window, which had become somewhat misted up, I could see that the land through which we were passing still had large tracts of winter snow, which had yet to be dispersed by the arrival of Spring.

The compartment door opened and the Okhrana man, Mr. Michailichenko looked in. "Gentlemen, our prisoners are due to depart, perhaps you would care to bid them farewell?"

Holmes and I followed him to the baggage compartment at the rear of the train, where, sat on packing cases, were our enemies. Shukin, tall and blond, Korbalov, shorter and bearded and Petrov, thin and balding, watched over by armed Okhrana men.

Shukin glared at Homes and myself. He shook a manacled fist and snarled at us. "You shall pay for this!" he said in English.

Sherlock Holmes looked mildly at the Russian. "Dear me," he said. "I was rather under the impression that it was yourself, rather than I who was about to pay."

The Russian jumped to his feet, his face a contorted mask of rage. Thankfully he was securely chained to the floor of the compartment, for had he not been so securely shackled, he surely would have struck Sherlock Holmes. Instead he contented himself with a stream of invective both in English and Russian. Then, visibly controlling himself, Shukin issued a final threat. "Our great leader will have his revenge on you. He has a long arm and it will reach whatever hole you crawl into and crush you."

Holmes threw back his head and laughed. "My dear Shukin. You are quite priceless."

Then suddenly his demeanour changed, gone was the hilarity and in its place, ice and steel. Holmes fixed the Russian with his piercing gaze and spoke in little more than a whisper. "Many have threatened to make an end to Sherlock Holmes. Your master will not be the first to do so, nor do I suppose him to be the last. He cannot succeed, because evil will never defeat good."

For a few moments Holmes held the hapless Shukin in his gaze, then turning abruptly upon his heel, he marched back along the train. "Come, Watson!" he cried over his shoulder. "We have no time to waste. A personage of far greater importance than these fellows awaits us and I have much to consider before that meeting."

When our train finally pulled into the great station at St. Petersburg, we had been travelling for nineteen long and weary hours. Mr. Michailichenko bade us farewell, he slowly shook hands with Holmes, Father Paul and myself, then like a general leading his troops into battle, he marched his prisoners away in the direction of the Peter and Paul fortress where they would be closely questioned about their crimes.

Sherlock Holmes and I collected our haversacks from the rack and stepped down onto the platform. A strong fresh wind was blowing through the high vaulted canopy sending discarded tickets into swirling eddies. Father Paul quickly followed, carrying his rather heavy Gladstone, and Andrews, who for his part was without baggage, brought up the rear.

As we made our way to the exit, I espied a shining black locomotive coupled to a number of sparkling royal blue carriages, each one emblazoned with a golden double eagle on the coachwork. "This is a most impressive train," I remarked.

"Indeed," agreed Father Paul. "It is the Imperial train. I expect that they are making ready for the Tsar's spring visit to the Crimea. Although I have never seen it before, I am told that it is appointed to the highest degree of luxury, befitting the stature of its noble passengers."

Recalling that back in 1860, I had seen the Royal train of Victoria and Albert, when they had visited the Epsom Derby, and the sharp pang of disappointment I had felt when unable to catch even the faintest glimpse of the interior, much less the august personages carried by the train, I vowed that this would be an opportunity too good to miss. I stepped up onto one of the platforms at the end of each carriage and peered inside.

"My dear fellow," said Holmes, half in amusement and half in exasperation. "You remind me of a child at the window of a confectioners with a penny in his hand. Do come down before you get yourself arrested."

As I looked into the interior of the carriage, my eager eye ran over the remarkable décor: the mahogany-panelled saloon fitted out with white furniture and, in the other carriage, a beautifully-appointed bathroom, resplendent with golden fittings.

It was at this juncture, I also espied two uniformed retainers of the Tsar making their way along the carriage towards me. Quickly I jumped back down to the platform and assisted my companions into a hurried exit, hoping all the while that I had not been observed snooping. As we passed into the square beyond, I smiled to myself and considered how it would have looked if my first encounter with His Majesty's Ambassador to Russia, Sir Angus Moule, had been through the bars of a prison cell, perhaps even the one next to Shukin and his associates.

After a short cab ride, Holmes, Father Paul, Andrews and I found ourselves at the Ambassador's private residence and waiting in the anteroom. The door opened and there stood the rotund figure of Sir Angus himself. "Good day to you, gentlemen," he said, shaking our hands warmly. "Notice of your impending arrival here in St. Petersburg was issued several weeks ago." He gazed quizzically at us. "I have been expecting you for some time, Mr. Holmes, Dr. Watson." He turned and smiled at Hunter Andrews. "My dear sir. I cannot say what an extraordinary pleasure it is to find you safe and well. I confess that we here at the embassy feared for your safe return. Yet here you are."

Andrews gestured in the direction of Holmes and myself. "It is due to the bravery and resourcefulness of my companions, that I stand here before you today. For without Mr. Holmes and Dr. Watson, I would be a prisoner still awaiting an unknown fate."

Sir Angus waved us to a row of chairs before the fire. Over tea, Sir Angus addressed himself to our mission. "Now that you have rescued Mr. Andrews, Mr. Holmes, your task must surely be at an end?"

Holmes looked sharply at the ambassador. "Indeed not, sir," he said. "Our mission is as yet only half completed. I believe that the liberty, if not the life of Tsar Nicholas may be in some peril." He took out the letter drafted by Patriarch Alexi. "I have here an introduction to Grand Duke Nicholas. In this note, the Patriarch explains his satisfaction with the veracity of my fears and implores the Grand Duke to give me every assistance in my investigation."

Sir Angus looked gravely at Holmes. "May I see the letter?"

Holmes nodded and handed the missive over. "You will observe that the note bears the Patriarch's seal," he said. "Father Paul has been sent with us as the Patriarchs personal emissary, to speak on our behalf if necessary and to alert the clergy in St. Petersburg to the Tsar's peril."

Sir Angus perused the letter, then he handed it back. He frowned and rubbed his furrowed brow. "Mr. Holmes, you will appreciate that it is not altogether an easy matter to obtain an interview with Grand Duke Nicholas. As commander of the Imperial army, he is a busy man and rarely grants interviews," he sighed. "You may have to wait for several days, before he will see you."

Sherlock Holmes fixed the ambassador with a gimlet eye. "Sir Angus. We have not travelled so many long and weary miles only to be obstructed by the vagaries of protocol and red tape." He smiled at Sir Angus, but there was no hint of humour in his eyes. "I am sure, however, if there is one man in St. Petersburg who can arrange an interview with Grand Duke Nicholas, then you are he."

The ambassador picked up the telephone receiver and dialled a number. There was a brief pause whilst the machinery connected his call, then a brief conversation, before the loud and rather gruff voice of the man whom we were seeking came on the line. Sir Angus and the Grand Duke spoke briefly in Russian, clearly exchanging pleasantries before Sir Angus got down to the purpose of his telephone call. The names of Sherlock Holmes and Dr. Watson were swiftly heard, followed by that of the Patriarch Alexi and finally that of Tsar Nicholas. It was at this point that the voice of the soldier was to be heard barking out an order. Sir Angus held out the receiver to Sherlock Holmes. "Mr. Holmes, the Grand Duke wishes to speak with you. Do not worry, his English is excellent."

Holmes took the receiver. "Good day, your Excellency … Yes, I am quite sure of my facts … Very good, sir. Doctor Watson and I would be pleased to meet you this evening … At seven o'clock this evening? We shall be there … Thank you, Sir … Goodbye."

He handed the receiver back to Sir Angus and smiled again. This time there was genuine humour in his eyes. "Well now, Watson," he said. "Not only are we summoned into the presence of Grand Duke Nicholas, we are also to dine with him. I hope that the gravity of the matter will not blunt your appetite?"

I smiled back. "My dear fellow, not even the announcement of the impending crack of doom would do that."

*****

It was a little before seven that evening when Sherlock Holmes and I were ushered into the private quarters of Grand Duke Nicholas. The rooms were plainly decorated and simply furnished with numerous mementoes of the Duke's military career festooning the apartment. The old soldier was sitting before a roaring fire. He stood up and smiled as we entered the room. The Duke was a tall, bearded man of perhaps sixty years, but he carried those years well!

"Gentlemen, welcome to St. Petersburg. The names of Sherlock Holmes and Dr. Watson are well known in Imperial circles." He turned and waved his hand at the book-lined walls of his study. "Your works, my dear Doctor, are to be found in many a library in Russia." He turned once more to face Holmes and myself. "Perhaps when you have a moment, sir, you would care to inscribe the volumes in my collection?"

"Gladly, sir," I replied, much delighted.

Sherlock Holmes looked sharply at me, but he kept his own counsel. Instead he reached into his pocket and produced the letter of introduction, which had proved to be the open sesame to the personage of the Tsar's cousin.

The old soldier's eyes lit up as they fell upon the seal of the Orthodox Church. He held out a huge, gnarled hand. "Ah, so this is the communication from my old friend, Patriarch Alexi?" He rumbled. "Tell me, Mr. Holmes, does his beard still reach down to his waist?"

Sherlock Holmes contemplated the old man, and they held each other in a frank gaze. "No, indeed, your Excellency," said Holmes. "As you know full well, the Patriarch's beard barely covers his chest, or, may I add, the small strawberry shaped birthmark on his neck."

The Grand Duke threw back his head and laughed loudly. "Capital, Mr. Holmes. You are no imposter." So saying, he tore open the envelope and read the contents quickly. At once, his face was transformed from jovial to grave. "Mr. Holmes, when Sir Angus spoke of your urgent mission, I had no inkling about its deep and serious nature. Tell me, what may I do to assist you?"

Briefly Holmes explained his profound fears for the safety of the Tsar. Grand Duke Nicholas nodded his grey head and looked worried. He spoke, however, with conviction. "This is all very well and good, Mr. Holmes, but for me to take action, you will need to furnish me with something of a solid nature."

Without replying, Holmes reached into another pocket, this time he produced the note that had been given to him by Captain Jefferson in Rome and which he had then carried assiduously with him since. He handed it to the Duke.

"Perhaps your Excellency would care to peruse this communication; whilst not in code, it is of a cryptic nature, and possibly with your particular knowledge of the Tsar's affairs, you may be able to shed some light on the more impenetrable passages."

He took the translation from his pocket, unfolded it and handed it to me with a terse request. "Here, Watson. Refresh your memory."

Once again I took the translation and read it through. It seemed to have been an absolute age and a whole world away, when sitting in the company of General James Wilton, Holmes and I had just read these words.

> S and M
>
> You will convey our volunteer into the hands of Mr R in Petersburg. Your passage through the region has been smoothed. Mischa and the Prince are on hand to assist you, if any problems arise. You will contact me in R for further instructions when your task is completed
>
> Good luck - VIU

"Vladimir Ilyich Ulyanov!" said the Grand Duke forcibly, his brow as black as thunder. "He is the Bolshevik we have been seeking these six years." He read the note through once more, rubbing his chin reflectively.

"Are you able to glean anything from the note, sir?" I asked tentatively.

"Let me see," said the old soldier slowly. "The volunteer, has to be your Mr. Andrews ... Mr. R ... Mischa and the Prince ... Hmm ..."

Suddenly his eyes seemed almost to explode, so wide did they open in wild disbelief. The Duke sat down heavily on an adjacent high-backed chair with an expression akin to that one might see on the face of a man who had been given the worst possible news about a medical condition. "I can hardly believe it," he said weakly. "No, this cannot be, it must not be."

The colour had drained completely from his handsome face. The note fell unnoticed from his fingers onto the table before him, whilst he stared into the middle distance with sightless eyes.

Quickly recognising the signs of shock, I moved over to the occasional table, by the fire and poured a stiff measure of brandy from the crystal decanter. I handed the glass to him and almost mechanically he took it and downed it in one gulp.

The brandy took a few moments to have an effect, then the Duke became simply galvanised. The colour returned to his cheeks and his eyes began to sparkle once more.

"Are you better, your Excellency?" I enquired.

"Quite better, " he replied. "But, by the stars, the people referred to in this note will not be feeling quite so well when I have finished with them!"

"I am sorry if I appear to be obtuse, sir," I said. "But you have clearly seen something in this communication which is indiscernible to Holmes and myself."

The old soldier looked at me and smiled grimly and gestured that Holmes and I should be seated. He held up the note once more. "You are exactly right, Dr. Watson. Although I can hardly believe it and unless I am sorely in error, the people referred to in this memorandum are none other than Rodzianko, the Imperial first minister of the Duma, Prince Felix Yousupov, a distant cousin to the Tsar and one of Russia's richest men ... and hardest of all to believe, Mischa ... the Tsar's younger brother."

I took a deep breath. Only now did the reason for the old man's great astonishment and upset become abundantly clear. Senior politicians and even the Tsar's own brother were plotting with a known revolutionary to overthrow him. Grand Duke Nicholas stood up and strode over to the fire, there he pulled the bell-rope for his servant. He looked defiantly at Holmes and myself.

"This is a serious and urgent matter, the nature of which must be conveyed to the Tsar immediately. Whilst you are preparing yourselves for dinner, I shall telephone him." The Duke surveyed us with keen grey eyes. "If you gentlemen are agreeable, I shall tell His Majesty that you will be accompanying myself to Tsarskoe Selo tomorrow morning, where I am certain he will desire you to place the matter before him personally."

A liveried servant appeared and the duke spoke briefly in Russian to him, before addressing Holmes and myself once more. "You are accommodated for the night?" he asked.

"Indeed," said Sherlock Holmes. "We are to stay with Sir Angus Moule at his private residence."

"Very good. Then I shall send a carriage around tomorrow morning at ten. Please be ready."

*****

The next morning Sherlock Holmes and I bade a fond farewell to Hunter Andrews. Sir Angus had succeeded in securing him a passage home with one of the returning embassy officials. A full set of clothes had been obtained, which would ensure that Andrews would make the journey dressed like the English gentleman he was. It was a crisp and clear morning and the young man was manifestly relieved to be able to pull on the heavy overcoat and don the wide-brimmed felt hat. "Goodbye, Mr. Holmes, Dr. Watson," he said. "I have only my profound gratitude with which to repay you for my life."

Holmes shook the departing Andrews's hand. "Think nothing of it, sir. Merely go home to your devoted wife and forget all about this most unpleasant episode."

Andrews climbed aboard the carriage and waved through the window to us. "Farewell!"

The driver goaded the horses into action and the vehicle sped off down the cobbled street. A stop at the junction, a turn to the right and Hunter Andrews was gone.

It was a little more than an hour later when a similarly attired Holmes and myself were on the road to Tsarskoe Selo, the Tsar's village situated some thirteen or fourteen miles to the south of the capital. Four people, Sherlock Holmes and I with our backs to the way we were travelling and Grand

Duke Nicholas and his personal aide, Mr. Littov, a retired cavalry officer, facing us, populated our carriage.

After exchanging the usual pleasantries, the Duke busied himself with a veritable mountain of paperwork. As the Grand Duke and Mr. Littov worked, our carriage ran through the streets of St. Petersburg. Across the wide river Neva we rattled, with the blue, yellow and white stucco fronts all glowing in the sun and the golden onion domes of the many churches glinting likewise. The feared Peter and Paul Fortress we saw to our right with its long red walls running nearly parallel to the river and its high golden tipped tower standing proudly above the city skyline.

Then swiftly, we passed through a poorer and greyer part of the city, before coming out onto the open highway and the lush green meadows with dark gloomy forests in the distance.

The Duke finally closed his case and sighed. His task for the present appeared to have been completed. "I am sorry, gentlemen," he said. "Unfortunately, the business of the Imperial Army is a never ending one, even now I have left much undone to escort you today." He leaned forward in his seat and addressed us in an almost conspiratorial manner. "I have left the army in the hands of General Sukhomlinov. He is a fool, but will take no precipitous action on his own initiative." The old soldier chuckled. "So it seems unlikely that war will be declared whilst my back is turned."

As our carriage rattled and bumped across the great St. Petersburg plain, a light snowfall danced and swirled about us on the biting wind and I for one, was particularly grateful for the heavy coats and fur hats with which Sir Angus had provided us.

Grand Duke Nicholas took out his watch and looked at it. He gave a grunt of satisfaction. "We shall be at our destination very soon, gentlemen. I will go immediately into conference with the Tsar. After lunch, I expect His Majesty will wish to interview you in person."

The road dipped and ran through a dark wood and then as we came back out into the sunlight a line of black, high railings began to run beside the road. Beyond I could see tall, bearded men on horseback. I prodded Holmes in the ribs.

"Cossacks," I murmured.

"This is the Imperial Park," said the Grand Duke. "The Cossacks guard the Tsar and his family. They are fierce, patriotic men exactly right for the task."

The carriage came to a halt before a pair of huge black and gold wrought iron gates, a Cossack in his red great-coat, his sabre at the ready, jumped down from his steed and peered suspiciously through the bars of the gate. When he recognised Grand Duke Nicholas, however, his demeanour changed. At once the gates were thrown open and we were waved through into the pleasure grounds beyond.

As the carriage rumbled along the drive, Grand Duke Nicholas pointed out many of the curious objects standing in the park. The obelisks, the monuments and the triumphal arches that so reminded me of Rome, and in some small part the grounds of Stourhead in Dorsetshire, placed in a larger arena.

"You are entering a retreat which very few will ever see," he remarked. "It is a pity that you are visiting at such an early stage of the year, because there are a number of splendid walks through many rare and interesting trees. Indeed during the Spring the perfume of the lilacs can be almost overpowering. But perhaps if time permits you will be able to visit the Chinese pagoda and the lake."

Eventually, the road brought us to the front of a magnificent blue and white rococo palace of immense size with golden onion domes and incredible ornamentation.

"This is the Catherine Palace," said the Duke. "It is named after Catherine the Great, although it was built by Elizabeth, the youngest child of Peter the Great. It is without doubt a rival to Versailles. The Tsar, however, does not particularly care for the palace and prefers to reside in the Alexander Palace, which, confusingly enough, was built by Catherine. As you will see in a few moments, it is as simple as the other is ornate."

We came through a high proscenium arch and before us stood the palace in question. Its simplicity of style and design was, to my eye, much to be preferred. The carriage came to a halt before a high gothic portal and our driver jumped down and rang the large brass bell by the entrance.

The doors were flung open and two large negro servants bowed to us. Behind them came two young serving women, one carried a large plaited loaf on a silver salver, the other held a silver pot of salt. Grand Duke Nicholas informed Holmes and myself that we should each break off a piece of bread and dip it into the salt. "It is a traditional Russian ceremony of welcome to visitors," he said waving us toward the young servants.

Then a graceful, clean-shaven man in his late forties appeared. He bowed low to the Duke and spoke briefly to him in Russian. He then smiled at Holmes and me and greeted us in English. "Mr. Holmes, Dr. Watson, I am Grand Duke Paul, the Tsar's uncle. Welcome to you both."

The Duke led us through a high vaulted entrance hall and up a flight of carved wooden stairs, then into a green drawing room furnished in a surprisingly modest fashion. A good fire was burning in the grate, before which I gladly warmed my hands.

"Now, gentlemen," he said briskly. "Grand Duke Nicholas and I will be busy for a while, so I trust you will make yourselves comfortable in the meantime."

We took off our outer garments and sat by the fire; the air of the room was remarkably sweet. "They are burning sandalwood," I murmured.

Suddenly, the door burst open and two small dogs of the spaniel breed came running in, barking and wagging their tails. They were swiftly followed by a dark-haired boy of perhaps nine or ten years. His headlong rush, however, was brought to an abrupt halt, when he realised that the room was inhabited by two strangers. "I beg your pardon, sirs," he said gravely in English, which I found surprising. "I had no idea that Papa had visitors."

Once again the door flew open and a pretty girl in her late teens burst in. She shouted in English. "Alexi, where are you, brother? You know what Mama has said about you running about like that? You must take care ... oh!"

For a brief moment we all stood silently, regarding each other. Holmes and myself by the fire and the two young people by the door, everyone embarrassed by the incident. Then, all at once, the spell was broken by the appearance of Grand Duke Nicholas.

"Oh, Uncle Nikki!" cried the girl. "We are so sorry. Are these gentlemen your friends?"

The old man spread his arms out and the children ran to embrace him.

"These gentlemen are my special friends from London," he said smiling. "They are Mr. Sherlock Holmes and Dr. Watson." The Duke looked fondly at them. "Mr. Holmes has urgent business with your papa."

He smiled again. "Gentlemen, let me introduce you to Alexis and Olga, the youngest and eldest of the Tsar's children."

The Duke placed a hand in the back of each of the royal children and gently guided them over to the fire. Olga curtsied and Alexis shook us by the hand.

"Dr. Watson," he said. "Mama is especially fond of your *Hound of the Baskervilles*. She says that the story embodies the ultimate victory of good over evil."

I smiled. "But do you like the story, Alexis?"

He shook his head. "No, sir, I find it much too scary."

"Now," said Grand Duke Nicholas sternly. "It is time for me to speak with my friends and high time you were washing and changing for luncheon." So saying he proceeded to propel the children and their dogs from the room. "Now, gentlemen, I have had a brief conversation with His Majesty, but pressure of work will prevent him from seeing you until this afternoon. I propose, therefore, that you lunch with me, then the Tsar will see you immediately afterwards."

*****

Luncheon, given the indubitable seriousness of our mission, proved nevertheless to be quite delightful. Although my military career was a part of the distant past, I discovered very quickly that Grand Duke Nicholas and I had much in common. As a consequence, tales of derring-do and old battles won and lost peppered our conversation and only half in jest did Holmes declare, all old soldiers to be incurable romantics.

After we had eaten our fill, it seemed quite appropriate to take our pipes and retire to the solarium and view the pleasure grounds from a warm and comfortable viewpoint. As I gazed idly at the vista, six figures appeared below, five young people and a grizzled and bearded man.

"It is Alexis and his sisters," said the Duke. "And I believe it is Derevenko who is accompanying them this afternoon."

"Why is it necessary for the children to be chaperoned?" Holmes asked him. "With the considerable security surrounding the Imperial family, I would have supposed it to be an unnecessary precaution."

"Ah! Then you do not know," said the Duke. "Derevenko does not watch over all the children, his task is to protect Alexis, whose special condition makes it necessary."

My interest was piqued. Then I recalled the admonition of the boy by his sister, as she cautioned him to be careful when running around. I wondered did he suffer from a condition known as brittle bone disease? I resolved to ask the Grand Duke the exact nature of the boy's condition.

"My dear, sir. What can it be that causes an apparently healthy boy to need constant supervision?"

Duke Nicholas sighed as he watched the frolicking children whom clearly he loved so dearly. As he replied his voice was quiet and thick with emotion. "Dr. Watson, my poor Alexis is afflicted by the scourge of haemophilia."

"The royal disease," I murmured.

"Indeed." Grand Duke Nicholas rose to his feet and stubbed out the remains of his cigar. "I shall go to the Tsar, now. I do not expect that he will keep you waiting very long."

Grand Duke Nicholas was gone for no more than five minutes, then, "Gentlemen. The Tsar will see you now."

The Duke led us down a wide corridor flanked by busts of the great and good, then down a short flight of stairs into a cul-de-sac where, at the far end, a high double door with a marble surround stood. Guarding the door was another of the Tsar's black servants, a tall muscular man.

The servant bowed low as we approached then he threw open the doors and gestured for us to enter. The Grand Duke led the way into a small antechamber, wainscoted and plainly furnished. The inner door was slightly ajar and the Duke looked into the room beyond. Immediately he signalled to Holmes and myself that we should follow him into the room. The inner chamber was large, well lit by high windows with heavy curtains and book-lined. In many ways it resembled the Duke's own quarters. Behind a large leather-topped desk sat the man we had travelled so many miles to meet; his Imperial Majesty the Tsar of Russia.

The Tsar stood up and smiled. "Gentlemen, you are welcome. Please sit down."

Sherlock Holmes wasted no time in detailing his concerns for the Tsar's safety. Now that he was in greater possession of the facts, Holmes was able to furnish the Tsar with a concise theory. Much of the discussion between Holmes and Sir Arthur Richardson on that cold early morning, at Cliff House, was aired and he made no bones about His Majesty's government's view. That unless fundamental changes were made at the heart of Europe's governments, then instability and worse would, like day and night, follow each other. The Tsar, however, whilst understanding the European dimension was at a loss to comprehend his own danger.

"But, Mr. Holmes," he objected. "Why should senior politicians and indeed members of my own family plot with known revolutionaries to have me removed? Why do they not come to me and tell me that for the good of the motherland, I should stand aside?"

"If asked, would you do so?" Holmes inquired.

"I would never consider it," the Tsar said flatly.

"Then would you consider commuting your absolutism into a constitutional monarchy?"

"Again, the answer has to be no."

Holmes sighed. "Well then, sir. I suggest that you have just answered your own question. If you are not open to persuasion, then they will resort to compulsion, possibly at the cost of your life."

"They would have me killed?" said the Tsar sharply. "Surely not?"

"I do not think for a moment that any of your politicians or relatives desire such an outcome, but they may believe that you will see the danger in which they are placing you and you will act in accordance with their wishes, therefore."

The Tsar grew red with anger and shook his head. "How little do they know me, Mr. Holmes. I could never agree to their demands whatever the cost. The Romanovs rule by divine right and I am prepared to die for that principle."

"Very well," said Holmes firmly. "If you will not discuss terms, then you must fight. Have them arrested and summarily executed as warning to those who would oppose you in the future."

The Tsar closed his eyes and rubbed his brow. He suddenly looked tired and ill.

"My dear sir," I said. "Are you unwell?"

"No, Dr. Watson. It is nothing. I am just a little overworked that is all."

He reached out for the carafe and poured himself a little water, but his hand was shaking so much, I feared that he would spill it. "Have you consulted your doctor, sir?" I enquired.

The Tsar drank the water and shook his head. "I have spoken to him on several occasions and each time he tells me that it is because I work too many hours and I should cut down on my work-load." He gestured at the pile of papers on his desk. "But how?"

Cognisant of losing the thread of his argument, Holmes continued. "Now, sir. You have heard my opinion about what you must do?"

The Tsar sighed and shook his head. "No, Mr. Holmes. I could never consent to the execution of members of my own family. Why, it would make me as bad as the Bolsheviks I have been opposing."

"Then what do you propose doing?"

The Tsar's answer never came, for without warning the door burst open and a tall swarthy man with long black hair and a large straggly beard rushed into the room. His eyes were large and luminous and held an almost hypnotic quality about them. He immediately spoke to the Tsar without waiting for introduction or indeed, acknowledgement of the presence of Holmes and myself. At the time I understood none of the conversation, save the urgent nature of the conversation. Later, a translation was offered to me by a third party.

"Little father, the boy is sick again."

"How so?" cried the Tsar jumping to his feet.

"Derevenko said that he fell when running after Tatiana by the lake."

The Tsar uttered a muted oath and almost pushed his visitor out of the way in his rush for the door. "Have you informed the Tsarina?" he shouted over his shoulder.

The bearded man answered in the affirmative then followed the swiftly disappearing Tsar into the corridor. Clearly an emergency of the first magnitude had occurred. The black servant then appeared in the doorway.

"Gents", he said. "Ah'm sorry you bin left alone like this, but when the boss hears bad news about the boy, he drops everything. But I 'spect he'll remember you soon."

I looked at the gentlemen who was addressing us in this fashion. He smiled at our obvious astonishment. "Guess you gents don't come across too many coloured folks from the U S of A? Partic'ly in the heart of Russia." He held out a huge hand. "Jim Hercules is m'name. How do you do?"

Sherlock Holmes shook his hand. "I have to confess, Mr. Hercules. You have surprised me," he said. "You are a surprise package, indeed. How have you come to be here in Russia?"

Mr. Hercules laughed a deep *basso-profoundo* laugh and told us of his journey from the son of a poor sharecropper in the southern States, through a remarkably successful career as an all-in-wrestler, to a wandering itinerant who had sailed for Europe on a whim. Then one day in Paris, he had been approached by agents of the Tsar, who recruited his services. "Well, gents. It seemed like the crazy sort of idea ah should go for, so go for it ah did, and here ah am." He laughed again. "Ah love it here, there's people from all over the world. There's even a few Russians too."

The study door opened once more and Grand Duke Nicholas looked in. "Where is His Majesty? I have just received an important communication from St. Petersburg."

Jim Hercules snapped immediately into his serving man persona and informed the Duke about the sudden departure of the Tsar and the probability that he would be found in the mauve-boudoir. In turn the Duke asked Mr. Hercules to escort Holmes and myself back to the green drawing room, but before we parted the Duke took Holmes aside and murmured something to him.

Back in the drawing room, we were left to our own devices. During our absence the fire had been made up and was burning merrily. I was much intrigued by the whispered words of Duke Nicholas. Holmes informed me, however, that the Duke had informed him only of the possibility of the plotters having a secret agent planted in the Tsar's household.

"We have a more serious problem, however," he said. "The very foundations which underpin the Imperial throne are under attack from the combined forces of politicians, Bolsheviks, even members of the Tsar's own family. All have joined together in an unholy alliance and his attention is elsewhere. The health of the Tsarina is also a constant worry and the Tsar himself appears to be ill," he shook his head. "Sadly, I believe that the family worries, he has heaped upon his shoulders are blinding him to the urgency of the action he must take to ensure that the Tsarevich for whom he cares so much has a throne to inherit."

But what are we to do?" I asked. "Because it seems to me that if there is no change in the *status quo* we may just as well pack our bags and go home."

"I do not think that such precipitous action would prove to be at all productive," said a voice from the doorway. I looked up from the carpet I had been studying morosely, to see Sir Angus Moule standing there.

"My dear fellow," said Holmes. "What brings you to Tsarskoe Selo?"

Sir Angus sat in a fireside chair. Warming his hands at the flames, he sighed contentedly. "It is bitter out today," he remarked. "At one stage of the journey I feared that I might freeze to death. The information I was carrying, however, was sufficient to warm even the coldest traveller."

"You have heard something to our advantages?" I asked.

Sir Angus looked about the room in a somewhat conspiratorial fashion. "It seems, gentlemen, that the Okhrana man, Mr. Michailichenko, has managed to elicit the fact that Ulyanov has somehow managed to infiltrate the royal household and, furthermore, has moved from his hiding place in Riga and has returned to St. Petersburg."

"Indeed," said Holmes. "Have you made this information available to the Tsar?"

Sir Angus looked aggrieved.

"Certainly, sir. Only a few minutes ago, I was speaking to Grand Duke Nicholas about the matter."

"I have to say how impressed I am by your thoroughness in this matter," I told him. "When you might have sent the message by courier, you came yourself."

Sir Angus chuckled.

"I have to tell you, Dr. Watson, that my actions have not been taken from the noblest of motives; The Tsar invariably treats his guests with overwhelming hospitality, an excellent meal with entertainment, followed by a nights accommodation, before breakfast and a sad return to St. Petersburg." He patted his extensive stomach. "As doubtless my ever expanding waistline will testify my visits are as frequent as protocol will allow."

"Was Mr. Michailichenko able to glean anything further from his captives?" I asked.

"Indeed. Apparently, Mr. Andrews was kidnapped with the sole purpose of gaining entry to the strong room at the Peter and Paul fortress, where much of the Imperial wealth is stored." He filled his pipe and lit it with a spill from the fire. "The finery you see about you is only the tiniest fraction of the Tsar's vast collection of ancient tapestries, furniture, ornaments and coin. If the Bolsheviks should get their hands on such a treasure trove, then they could finance a private army any nation might fear."

"We must be thankful that good fortune enabled us to prevent them from fulfilling their plans," said I. I laughed. "How ironic, then, that they have been incarcerated in the very place they were seeking to burgle."

"The Tsar," said Holmes suddenly. "Does he regularly provide entertainment for visitors?"

"Yes indeed," replied Sir Angus. "He will regularly invite close friends and important visitors. The gatherings are usually as intimate as they are lavish."

Holmes stood up. Throwing his cigarette into the fire he proceeded to pace up and down, his face drawn into a mixture of deep thought and repressed excitement. "A soirée," he said at last. "The Tsar must give a soirée. Only on this particular occasion, it will be I, and not His Majesty, who will be drawing up the invitations." He looked at me and smiled his brief smile. "But we must make it public, Watson. We must make it very public indeed."

*****

The morning dawned, both bright and clear. As I lay in my bed, shafts of sunlight streamed in through the tall windows and lit up the pale green walls of the room. Despite the deep comfort of my sleeping accommodation, however, I was keen to be up and about.

At breakfast, Sherlock Holmes was deep in a newspaper. "Good morning, Watson. I have here the news from home," he held up the paper and I saw that he was holding a copy of *The Daily Mail*. "Although the news is somewhat out of date, it is a welcome memento of home nevertheless." He turned to the back page and chuckled. "Here we are, my boy. As a sportsman, you will appreciate this article. On Saturday last the Boat Race was abandoned when both teams had their crafts sink from under them, resulting in postponement of the race until Monday, the day this edition was published. So the result unfortunately is not yet to hand."

"Speaking of races," I said. "Is there news of Captain Scott's race to the Pole?"

He turned the pages until the article he was seeking came to hand. "It would seem that Amundsen has won the race. A report filed from Tasmania says that his party arrived on December the fourth, but nothing has been heard from Scott, however."

Breakfast being over, Holmes and I retired to the fire to drink our coffee. Grand Duke Nicholas looked in, he appeared to be somewhat more relaxed than previously. Alexis, it transpired, had woken up feeling quite well, the Tsar, as a consequence, was also in an excellent mood.

"I require a lock of hair from the Tsar and the Tsarina," said Holmes without preamble.

Grand Duke Nicholas looked sharply at Holmes, his face registering incredulity. "You are not serious, Mr. Holmes?" he growled. "No. It is quite impossible, even for someone so respected as yourself."

"I am perfectly serious, sir. I can assure you, that the hair is required so that I may experiment upon it for traces of ... poisoning."

"Poisoning?"

"Indeed, it is my belief that small quantities of a substance have been introduced into the food and drink of the Tsar and Tsarina. If so, a simple chemical test will confirm or deny my suspicions."

The Duke looked at Holmes with wide eyes. "Can this be true?" he said weakly.

"Quite, true," I assured him. "The symptoms recently shown by their Majesties betray all the hallmarks of poisoning. A general lethargy, sickness, a loss of appetite and changes in their skin texture, indeed many of these symptoms were plain to see in the Tsar yesterday."

Duke Nicholas sat down heavily on a high-backed chair. He waved his hands as if trying to push the argument away. "I cannot believe it", he said. "Someone in the Imperial household is poisoning the Tsar?" Suddenly the Duke rose to his feet. "If it is your considered opinion, Mr. Holmes, then I must believe you."

"Very good," said Holmes, rising to his feet also.

"Watson," he said turning to me. "I expect that you will be able to amuse yourself whilst I attend to these matters?"

"I expect so, Holmes," I said wearily. "The newspapers look very interesting."

"Excellent." He opened the door for the Duke.

"Chemicals," he said. "And a list of those servants with access to the Tsar's food and drink."

"Of course, Mr. Holmes. I will see what can be done."

Then they were gone.

I did not see Sherlock Holmes until after luncheon, when he came in followed by a servant who was carrying a large box. When the man had departed Holmes held up two glass phials he had been carrying. "Samples of hair taken from the dressing tables of the Tsar and Tsarina," he said. "Once again, I owe a debt of gratitude to our friend Mr. Hercules. He was able to persuade their Majesty's personal maid, Galina and valet, Yanulov, to make their hairbrushes available for my inspection."

I opened the box and peered in. It was full of jars containing various chemicals, glass tubes and other paraphernalia. "It is part of a chemistry set belonging to the Tsarevich," said Holmes. "He was given a large and expensive one last Christmas, but has shown little interest in it, so I have borrowed a part for my experimentation."

"My dear fellow, you never cease to surprise me."

Holmes laughed. "The Tsar said as much when I spoke to him earlier and asked him to arrange a soirée and to invite only the people on the list I handed him."

"He has agreed?" I asked.

"Indeed."

"What of the poisoner?"

"I refrained from mentioning the matter, but with the assistance of Mr. Hercules, I was able to interview all servants who are intimately involved with the production and delivery of the Tsar and Tsarina's comestibles. However, let me commence to experiment, then, depending on the outcome, I may be closer to an opinion."

Seven

Two complete days had passed since the arrival at Tsarskoe Selo of Sherlock Holmes and myself. The children of the Tsar had departed, along with Derevenko to the Imperial yacht at Lyvadia, on the Black Sea. Now a third day had dawned. Holmes had laid his plans and they were cut and dried. Each of the presumed conspirators was in receipt of an invitation to a small, but exclusive, soirée. The entertainment was to include questioning about their machinations by Holmes, followed by an even more uncomfortable interview with the Tsar.

Considerable thought had gone into the matter and it was arranged that others, quite unconnected with the intrigue, would also be invited, less those who plotted with the Bolsheviks should grow suspicious and refuse the invitation.

I saw little of Holmes that morning, he had much to discuss with the Tsar. It was not an uninteresting time, however, for I spent a good deal of the morning observing the number of arrivals and departures. Vans stuffed to the gunwales with provisions, a dozen or more liveried servants and finally, several carriages containing musicians carrying their instruments as if they had been constructed from eggshells; all employed to ensure the success of the evening.

At last, Holmes appeared. He looked worried. "Things are moving fast, Watson," he said. "Reports of trouble in the Siberian gold fields have been filed. Duke Nicholas telephoned the Tsar to warn him that mass meetings, undoubtedly stirred up by Bolshevik agents, might lead to trouble. He has an army battalion standing by, but he is very concerned that news of this strike could lead to similar outbreaks in St. Petersburg and other towns and cities."

"But I do not understand," I said. "Surely the people of Russia are not so discontented, that news of a strike would promote unrest?"

"If the Bolsheviks have anything to do with it, then trouble is guaranteed," he said. "It seems that Ulyanov has an agent in every town and city prepared for such an eventuality. In St. Petersburg the agent is thought to be Joseph Djugashvili. Thanks to the Okhrana, however, his whereabouts and the alias under which he is travelling are known. So, perhaps he will be arrested before he can act. Let us hope fervently that my plans bear fruit and the Tsar may act with speed and sagacity, thereby undermining at least a part of the general conspiracy facing him. Then, perhaps he will be able to turn his mind to the European question."

"It would seem that he is being squeezed by two giant forces," I said. "Either of which might overwhelm him."

"Just so," said Holmes. "I am very afraid, however, that he will have neither the character, nor the understanding of the peril in which he finds himself, to take the urgent decisions necessary to ensure the continuation of the monarchy, or indeed, avoid conflict in Europe."

Then, at last, the evening of the soirée was at hand. The Tsar had declared that the event should take place in the Amber Room at the Catherine palace, so Holmes took some little time in inspecting the venue during the afternoon; and when he returned to our quarters, he pronounced himself to be satisfied with the arrangements. "The room is perfect for our requirements, Watson," he declared. "The windows will be shuttered from the outside during the evening and there is only one exit, which has double doors and a lock stout enough to withstand all but the most determined assault."

It was a little before seven when there came a knock at our sitting room door, thinking it was the servant with my hot water, I stepped into my room and called out for him to enter and place the jug upon the washstand next to my bed. From behind me and much to my surprise, there came a deep throaty chuckle and the voice of Grand Duke Nicholas. "Certainly, sir," he said. "Do you wish me to shave you now, sir?"

"My dear fellow," I cried, spinning around upon my heel. "Please forgive me. I had no idea."

The Duke laughed. "No harm done, Dr. Watson," he said. "Now I have something for you."

The Duke held out a large flat cardboard box he had been carrying under his arm. "Now, sir. As you are a military man, the Tsar thought that you might care to wear the uniform of the Imperial army at supper tonight."

I took the box and opened it to discover a superb dark blue dress uniform. Stammering my profound delight at such a single honour, I enquired just how I had earned the right. The Duke brushed aside my flow of thanks and explained that it was the Tsar's desire to honour me in some small way for my felicity. "The insignia is of a rank equivalent to your British army captain," he said. "It is the uniform worn by all Imperial army doctors, so it is all quite appropriate."

So it was, that a few minutes later, I appeared before Sherlock Holmes, who himself was attired in white tie and tails, another gift from the Tsar.

"My dear fellow," he cried as he caught sight of me. "You are a credit to both their majesties, King George and Tsar Nicholas."

"Thank you, Holmes," I replied cheerfully.

"Now, my boy," he said, reverting to his usual persona. "Do not forget to slip your service revolver into your tunic, for tonight, I fear we may have need of it," he smiled briefly as he collected his own revolver from the drawer. "Very well, on with the motley, Watson."

*****

It had been my expectation that we should walk the short distance between the Alexander Palace and the Catherine

Palace, but when Holmes and I stepped out into the night air, a carriage was awaiting us.

The short drive completed, we arrived at the grand entrance to Rastrellis's magnificent creation. The Palace was ablaze with light and colour and once inside the huge marble hall, we were greeted by an enormous bearded Cossack, resplendent in his red and gold uniform, who raised his sabre in a salute. He signalled to one of the negro servants and as the man approached, I recognised him to be Jim Hercules.

"Evenin', gents," he said quietly.

"You know what you have to do?" Holmes asked him.

"Yes, sir. I know."

Mr. Hercules led us across the marble hall in the direction of the music. Down a long red and gold corridor we walked, our footsteps echoing on the marble floor. Then he threw open some double doors and bowed Holmes and myself into the Amber Room and a sight never before equalled anywhere in Europe.

Over a long lifetime of travel and adventure, I have called upon many of the most important people in Europe and beyond and have been entertained in the most sumptuous surroundings in their splendid palaces and houses, but nothing could have prepared me for the magnificence of the amber room. Even now I have considerable difficulty in describing adequately the golden honey coloured walls; excepting the high windows and huge gilded mirrors, the room was covered entirely in amber. Above, hung many crystal chandeliers aglow with a thousand candles and at each end of the room there stood an enormous fireplace piled high with yet more sandalwood perfuming the room.

I looked around with wide eyes, then at Holmes and I addressed him in tones usually reserved for the holy places of this world. "Is it not magnificent?" I said.

"Magnificent indeed."

It was then when I turned my attention to the assembled guests and the chamber orchestra playing the music of Strauss, Von Suppe and other popular composers. Before the orchestra stood a row of white chairs placed in preparation for the evening's entertainment. Down the middle of the room stood the dining table simply groaning with table furniture, gold, silver and crystal. Then, at the farthest end of the room there stood two tables festooned with bottles of the finest wines.

Grand Duke Paul, the Tsar's uncle, stepped forward to greet us. "Gentlemen, you are welcome. Please come and meet the Tsar."

The Duke led Holmes and myself along a line of many of the most prominent and august personages in Imperial Russia. In turn, I shook hands with the Tsar, who commented on the excellent fit of my uniform, the Tsarina, Grand Duke Michael (Mischa), Grand Duke Nicholas, who grasped my hand warmly and Grand Duchess Sonia, the Tsar's sister, pale and morose, (I was later informed that she was pining for her husband, who had accompanied the Imperial children to the Crimea).

After a short interlude, the assembly was called to the table. Sherlock Holmes and I were seated opposite each other. To my left was the silent Grand Duchess Sonia, whom I cannot recall uttering a single sentence. To my right sat a Dr. Zhitomirsky, a large bearded man, whom in direct contrast to the Duchess, never seemed to stop talking.

Holmes was placed between Grand Duke Michael and the renowned Konstantin Stanislavsky, director of the Moscow Art Theatre.

As I gazed along the table, I espied the other supposed plotters, Prince Felix Youssupov, who was seated opposite the Grand Duke Nicholas and Minister Rodzianko, who sat to his right.

Dinner was taken off the famous 'frog service'. Dr. Zhitomirsky, discerning my own medical credentials, immediately deluged me in a positive avalanche of small talk. He told me that the 'frog service', was commissioned by the Empress Catherine from Wedgewood and it consisted of some nine hundred pieces. As the wine was served he remarked about the fineness of the Bordeaux.

"Chateau Lafite; 1896, I believe," he said tasting the wine. "But wait until you drink the 1893 Hock. I believe that the Tsar himself chose it after visiting Queen Victoria at Windsor Castle."

I listened patiently to the talkative Doctor, who seemed to have an opinion on everything. Then, just as my patience began to evaporate, his ear was caught by Duke Nicholas. Thankful for the aural respite, I looked across the table at Sherlock Holmes who seemed to be deep in animated conversation with Duke Michael and Mr. Stanislavsky. Observing my interest, he brought me into the conversation. "Watson, Mr. Stanislavsky is interested in bringing our adventures to the Russian stage. What do you think of that my dear fellow?" he said.

The impresario nodded. "Indeed, Dr. Watson. Perhaps I can do for Russia, what Mr. William Gillette has done for America and Europe. Perhaps later we may discuss the matter?"

Then Dr. Zhitomirsky was talking to me again. By now, he had exhausted his store of medical anecdotes and opinions on the wines of the world, he turned, therefore, to the reason for my visit to St. Petersburg.

Cognisant of the need for discretion, I felt somewhat nonplussed about how I should answer his question, when fate in the shape of Brother Grigory intervened. The double doors flew open and the priest staggered into the room shouting at the top of his voice. He pushed, Yanulov, the Tsar's valet, out of the way.

"Little father!" he cried. "Why do you waste your time on these fools? Who are they anyway? Jackals feeding at the table, little father." He lurched towards the Tsar thrusting aside the servants waiting on the table, before coming to a swaying halt before his master. "Look at them," he shouted waving his hands. "Traitors! Plotters! How can you sit down with those who would overthrow you, little father? Why do you not have them arrested for treason?"

There was a sharp intake of breath from many of the guests and none sharper than the intake of John H. Watson. The drunken ranting of Brother Grigory had not only unsettled many guests, they had also undone the plans laid so carefully by Sherlock Holmes. Gazing at the Tsar I saw him to be pale and visibly embarrassed.

Grand Duke Paul was the first to react to the priests drunken outburst. He jumped from his seat and grasped Brother Grigory by the arm and almost dragged him away from the Tsar's side. At a signal from the Duke two of the black bodyguards seized the swaying priest and quickly hauled him from the room.

Dr. Zhitomirsky poked me in the ribs and muttered into my ear.

"Pah! That Grigory, he is Rasputin! Dissolute. The Tsar is a fool to trust him. One day he will betray one secret too many."

The Tsar rose to his feet and the general hubbub caused by this most remarkable interlude died down. "My friends, please do me the honour of accepting my profound personal apology. Brother Grigory does not know what he is saying. You are all my friends and let us drink, therefore, to that friendship." He clapped his hands and Yanulov set to opening magnums of champagne with the consequential popping of corks.

Dr. Zhitomirsky leaned over once more. "Louis Roederer … Crystal. The Tsar's best."

He held up his glass to have it charged, took a sip and pronounced it to be excellent. He then returned to the matter of Brother Grigory. "That drunken priest. No state secret is closed to him. The Tsarina dotes on him and the Tsar relies upon his opinion on everything."

I looked at the Doctor with surprise. "Surely you are joking?" I replied. "You cannot know as much."

"Indeed?" he replied. "I know a great deal more about political matters in this country than you might think," he tapped his nose, knowingly. "For example, I know that Sherlock Holmes and Dr. Watson are not in St. Petersburg merely for the good of their health." He held up his glass for yet another refill. "Would it surprise you, Dr. Watson, if I told you that one of the Bolsheviks is serving here tonight?"

"Here!" I cried, sitting up sharply in my seat and almost spilling my drink. "You are mistaken."

He smiled, his eyes disappearing beneath pink rolls of fat. "Do not concern yourself, sir. I am on your side. The man in question is presently pouring wine for the Tsarina."

I carefully scrutinised the servant. He was quite short and somewhat Asiatic looking. He had a swarthy, pock-marked skin and black, spiky hair as well as an ample moustache.

"He is Djugashvili, or Stalin, as he likes to be known. That means 'man of steel'."

I looked about me, but none of the others at the table seemed to be focussing on our conversation. Dr. Zhitomirsky placed a hand upon my arm. "Djugashvili is the Bolsheviks most senior agent in St. Petersburg. He must be here under the direct orders of his master."

"Ulyanov?"

"Indeed. Or Lenin as he is known to his cohorts."

"Then you are aware of the threat to the Tsar?"

"Of course. Is that not the reason why Youssupov and Rodzianko were invited here tonight?"

I sighed. Apparently, Holmes's subterfuge was not quite the secret it might have been. I enquired of the doctor how it was he had come by the information.

Zhitomirsky laughed. "Sir, I am the fellow from whom the original news of Bolshevik sedition has come. I am the *agent provocateur* in this affair. The Bolsheviks believe that I am a renegade and a traitor, whilst, in fact, I am working for the state. Only last week I reported the arrival of Djugashvili in St. Petersburg to the Okhrana."

"Then are you aware of the possible trouble in Siberia?"

"No. I was not told about that. But it would explain his presence. He is undoubtedly here to stir up sedition."

"Do you know what Holmes's intentions are here tonight," I asked.

He nodded. "Grand Duke Nicholas, he is the one to whom I report, he told me yesterday. He also told me that I should not become involved directly if trouble was to break out, I should take cover."

I felt for the revolver securely tucked into my tunic. "Perhaps you should quickly take the Duke's advice, Doctor," I said. "Because I am not too certain that the musical event will ever commence. Either Sherlock Holmes or the Bolsheviks must act very soon, I think."

Before I could speak further the Tsar and the Tsarina stood up. This was a signal that the dinner was at an end and all guests should do likewise. The Tsar spoke quietly to one of the servants who in turn signalled to the orchestra that it should commence to play. The Imperial couple walked from their seats at the table and towards their seats in the row of white chairs before the dais.

Sherlock Holmes, I discovered talking to Grand Duke Paul and Mr. Stravinsky. They were discussing Stravinsky's music. The composer sounded enthusiastic. "My dear Duke," he said. "You will discover very soon that I am writing something that will set the world on fire. I call it *The Rite of Spring* and tonight I propose to conduct some passages from the work."

I caught Holmes by the sleeve. "My dear fellow, I have something to tell you."

He nodded and excused himself from the conversation. "Watson," he said. "Why the worried expression?"

"It is Dr. Zhitomirsky."

He chuckled. "I understand, old fellow. He has driven you to distraction with his incessant chatter."

"No, indeed," I said sharply. "He has driven me to distraction with his profound knowledge about the matter we are facing before us tonight."

In my long association with Sherlock Holmes I cannot recall astonishing him so, or if I have he has hidden it very well. On this occasion, however, he appeared momentarily floored.

Dr. Zhitomirsky had placed himself at the far end of the row, he was seated next to Grand Duke Nicholas. Holmes crouched down between them and began an earnest conversation. After a few moments the Doctor stood up and made his way towards the exit.

"Well done, Watson," said Holmes as he rejoined me. "Dr. Zhitomirsky is indeed in the pay of the Imperial authorities, Grand Duke Nicholas has confirmed as much. It also appears that we may be about to witness the unmasking of a counter plot by the Bolsheviks."

"But what shall we do about Djugashvili?"

"You have your revolver to hand, Watson?"

It was then, as Holmes questioned me, that pandemonium broke out in the room. The man Dr. Zhitomirsky had identified as Djugashvili pulled out a pistol from his tunic and fired it into the air. He shouted something in Russian and moments later the doors burst open, literally knocking the black bodyguards to the floor. A group of five or six men dressed in palace livery, each one brandishing a weapon, crashed into the room shouting at the top of their voices.

The room was filled with the oaths of men, the screaming of the ladies and the crashing and smashing of overturned furniture. Several gunshots pierced the noise and panicking guests were throwing themselves in all directions in an attempt to avoid injury.

Then there came the sound of a single gunshot quite close behind me and I saw the flying figure of Sherlock Holmes and the shattering of a windowpane exactly where he had been standing seconds before.

Suddenly Jim Hercules was beside me. He grabbed my arm and shouted in my ear. "Quick, Dr. Watson. Help me overturn this table!"

The black ex-wrestler needed little assistance from me, however, for with one mighty heave, he sent the table crashing to the floor, sending the table furniture crashing and scattering in all directions. Immediately several of the guests threw themselves into the lee of the table. I noted that Prince Yussupov and Rodzianko were among the first so to do.

"Arthur!" It was the voice of the Tsar. "Send for the Cossacks." The other black bodyguard dropped the Bolshevik he was attacking and made a quick exit.

A burst of gunfire showed that the forces of good were hitting back. Holmes and Grand Duke Nicholas were firing at the Bolsheviks, two of whom were put out of action immediately. Then Jim Hercules picked up one of the empty champagne magnums, grasping it firmly, he swung it around his head like a club and one of the Bolsheviks was sent spinning to the floor.

"Who said champagne wasn't a hard drink," he cried as he hurled it into the face of another of the Tsar's enemies. He turned to me and laughed. "It's a good thing that the Tsar's bottles are unbreakable, or they'd be too expensive to use!"

Then just as suddenly as it had begun, the violence ceased. The Bolsheviks, nonplussed at the vigour of our response appeared simply to simply lose heart. For one thing, only Djugashvili and one other was armed with a pistol, and for another, they were woefully disorganised. But from the window there came a splintering and crashing noise. Somebody outside was ripping open the shutters. The glass shattered and a ladder appeared from the void. At a signal from Djugashvili the survivors began to scramble through the window and into the cold night air beyond.

As he reached the ladder the Bolshevik leader turned and shouted in Russian; then he was gone with his comrades.

I was tempted to fire upon the retreating men, but Holmes calmly dissuaded me. "Let them go, Watson. They will not escape, the Cossacks will see to that."

I looked out into the darkness of the pleasure grounds, but could see nothing. Instead I turned my attentions to the chaos which reigned within. Two Bolsheviks lay dead on the floor, whilst another was slumped unconscious against the wall. Everyone, with the noble exception of Holmes, Grand Duke Nicholas and Jim Hercules was peering warily over the edge of the upturned dining table.

Yet, in the middle of this incredible scene of chaos and disaster, the chamber orchestra was playing as if nothing untoward had occurred.

Sitting on perhaps the only upright chair, I looked at Holmes and began to smile. Clearly in his mind he also saw the incongruity of the situation and he began to laugh. Others coming up for air also noticed the music and they too joined in the hilarity and before long the entire room was ringing to the sound of uproarious laughter.

The doors flew open and the huge Cossack chief stood there his eyes wide with amazement at the chaos and the dozen or so people laughing fit to burst. He must have though us all to be quite mad! Then upon his shouted command a dozen bearded men of his regiment poured into the room. The Tsar shouted to him that the Bolsheviks had escaped through the window and the Cossack leader urged his troops onward into the darkness.

As I looked out onto the pleasure grounds once more, I could see lights and the distinct outline of figures running in all directions, then sounds of gunfire and flashes of light; clearly the Bolsheviks had fallen foul of the Tsar's Cossacks who had determined themselves to take no prisoners.

At last the room was beginning to return to some resemblance of order. Now that the danger had passed, the Tsar and Tsarina took command of the evening once more. The table was reset upon its legs and at once the servants set about the task of clearing up the debris. Fine Napoleon brandy was ordered by the Tsar for those who would take it and the gentlemen were permitted to smoke. The Emperor stood upon the dais and addressed the assembly. "My friends. This has been an ... interesting evening. Fortunately we have all escaped without injury. I propose, therefore, that we should continue to enjoy the music. If Mr. Stravinsky will perform? But those who desire to retire may do so now. I will send lights with you as soon as my Cossacks report to me that all is well. Those who wish to stay may join me in taking some refreshment."

Those who desired to retire included the Tsarina and the Grand Duchess Sonia while Dr. Zhitomirsky, who had by now appeared from whatever hiding place he had found stayed. However, Mr. Stanislavsky and Sir Angus, who excused himself on the grounds of making an early start the next morning took their leave. Those who doubtless harboured a strong desire to depart, but did not dare so to do were the Grand Duke Michael, Mr. Rodzianko and Prince Felix Youssupov. The Grand Duke in particular looked pale and shocked, but the Tsar grasped him firmly by the arm and led him over to the row of chairs now rearranged by the fire.

Soon the shutters had been replaced and a heavy curtain was draped across the shattered window, consequently a semblance of warmth was returning to the room. Also joining the guests by the fire was Jim Hercules, invited to stay at the expressed request of Sherlock Holmes. The part he had played in the routing of the Bolsheviks decreed that he was well deserving of such an honour.

The Tsar looked sharply at the departing servants before addressing the assembly, or at least those who were worthy of his scorn. "Youssupov, Rodzianko ... Mischa. Do you hate me so much that you would consort with such villains? Tell me, what part have you played in this dastardly act?"

There came a chorus of denials from the would-be plotters, but the Tsar held up his hand for silence. He signalled to Grand Duke Michael that he should speak. The Grand Duke gazed at him pleadingly. "Brother, there was no plot, tonight. Whilst it is true that we have consulted with agents of the Bolsheviks, we did not know that they would take the matter into their own hands. I swear by the holy mother church, this was not our doing."

Then Rodzianko spoke up. "That is so, your Imperial Majesty. We have used Dr. Zhitomirsky as our messenger. As you know he is the Okhrana agent closest to their organisation. But I swear also that we know nothing about tonight. Our association with the Bolsheviks was meant only to intimidate you into acceding to our request for a new direction for Russia."

The Tsar looked at the Prime Minister; real anger was registered in his eyes. "Can this be true?" he said sharply. "You are merely the victims of circumstances?"

Sherlock Holmes stood up and addressed the Tsar. "Your Majesty. Perhaps there is truth in what they say. Is it possible that another was privy to our plans and has engaged in idle talk before friends of the Bolsheviks?"

The Tsar shook his head. "No, Mr. Holmes. That is quite impossible."

Holmes persisted, however. "How many were admitted to the circle of knowledge?"

"Myself, Grand Duke Nicholas, Dr. Zhitomirsky, Dr. Watson and yourself, Mr. Holmes."

"And there is no-one else with whom you have discussed the matter?"

The Tsar appeared a little nettled by Holmes's continuing questions, but he answered nevertheless. "Only Brother Grigory, I asked his opinion ..."

He was interrupted by an angry exclamation from Dr. Zhitomirsky. "Rasputin!" he cried, jumping to his feet. "That dog. His drunken display this evening should have warned me of his treachery. It is your precious friend, your Majesty, who had betrayed us."

Prince Youssupov also spoke up. "It must be he, dearest cousin. For only last Thursday, I saw him in the very tavern frequented by traitors and seditionist when I was on my way to Nevsky Prospect to meet a friend. He was shouting and swearing that these insects would be squashed by the might of the Tsar. Then he was thrown out. It was only by crossing the road and retracing some of my footsteps that I succeeded in avoiding him. I wish to God now that I had taken more notice of his words."

"The drunken fool," growled Grand Duke Nicholas slapping his leg angrily.

"There is your culprit without question," said Holmes. "Perhaps he was not intending to betray our intrigue, but he seems to have done precisely that."

"I will kill him!" cried Prince Youssupov.

"Nobody will kill anyone," said the Tsar quietly but firmly. "I see it all now ... It has all been a ghastly mistake." He spread his hands out before him in a gesture of resignation. "We have all been guilty of lapses of judgement. Brother Grigory, Mischa, Felix, Mr. Rodzianko and myself. Therefore I propose that we forget the whole matter." He stood up. "Gentlemen, perhaps we should adjourn for tonight."

The assembly stood up also. The Tsar looked tired and worn. He put an arm around the shoulder of Grand Duke Michael and another around the waist of Grand Duke Nicholas and addressed us for the final time that night. "Let us to bed and in the morning we may make more sense of this convoluted matter."

The double doors opened and the Tsar and his supporters disappeared into the corridor. In a very few moments only Sherlock Holmes and I remained in the room. Holmes picked up the last unopened bottle of Louis Roederer Crystal and gently eased out the cork. He filled two glasses and held one out to me, the other he raised in a toast.

"Bolsheviks and royalists. A plague on both their houses," he said wearily.

I raised my glass in return. "And confound them equally," I said.

*****

It was not until the debris of breakfast had been cleared away that Sherlock Holmes pronounced upon the events of the night before. The day had dawned cool and wet and Holmes stood in the solarium watching the raindrops run in little rivulets down the glass.

"You know, Watson," he said after a long silence. "Last night was a quite remarkable and unsatisfactory affair. Indeed I believe that this morning we have more questions than solutions." He paused momentarily to re-light his pipe before continuing. "For example, I would very much like to know how the Bolsheviks managed to infiltrate the caterers so easily. I am also keen to discover exactly how Djugashvili was able to avoid detection for so long and why, if the Okhrana was carefully observing his activities, did they allow him so much freedom of movement?"

I nodded in agreement. There were several unanswered questions bothering me too. "I would like to know just how

Djugashvili managed to escape last night," I said. "You have indicated that there is someone in the Imperial household who is a traitor." I leaned forward and threw my cigar into the fire. "Did this person assist the Bolsheviks to escape? Indeed, Holmes, is it Brother Grigory?"

Holmes shook his head. "I do not believe Brother Grigory to be guilty of deliberate disloyalty. His fault lies in his proclivity towards loose talk brought on by an over indulgence of alcohol. Indeed it is the Tsar whom I would blame for allowing the priest so much licence."

"Priest, we call him," I said. "How can such a man wear the cloth?"

"It appears that he is part of a sect which is persuaded that, if God forgives our sins, then the greater the sin, the greater the forgiveness," he smiled briefly. "I cannot say, however, that it is a doctrine to which I would subscribe."

I shook my head in disbelief at the situation into which the Tsar seemed to have got himself. As for the traitor, Holmes was not prepared to give him a name, at least for the present. Clearly understanding that I should get precisely nowhere and the avenue I was presently travelling down was a cul-de-sac, I turned instead to the matter of Grand Duke Michael, Prince Youssupov and Mr. Rodzianko. It appeared, upon the face of it, that the Tsar was prepared to give the plotters the benefit of the doubt and was minded to call their involvement with the Bolsheviks an indiscretion.

"It seems to me, Holmes that there is very little point in remaining here now. The Bolsheviks's plot has been uncovered, likewise the plotting of the Tsar's own people. The attempt to kill the Tsar has been foiled. Only the liberty of Djugashvili and his master, Ulyanov, now remains a problem. If we are unable to unmask the traitor in the Imperial household, then we have done here all we may do."

Holmes slapped me upon the shoulder and laughed. "Watson, always the man of action. But you are quite right, my boy. We have done nearly all that we came here to do. The authorities will have to attend to the Bolsheviks, but I believe that we can unmask the traitor before we return home. Indeed, I have formulated a plan to do exactly that."

"Are any of the friends of the Tsar involved?" I enquired.

"No. It is as the Tsar has inferred. They acted from the highest of motives, when attempting to persuade him to modify his position, even if they in the process became involved with the basest of individuals. It is someone quite different whom we are seeking."

"But you will not tell me who it is?"

Holmes regarded me with a mischievous twinkle in his eye. "Not yet, Watson. Not yet."

Holmes can be infuriating when he has discovered something quite unnoticed by others. I believe it to be the frustrated actor in him that drives him to keep the undiscovered facts to himself. Only when he believes the time to be ripe, will he puncture the bubble of mystery in which he has surrounded himself and let the truth escape. Perhaps it is Holmes, rather than Stanislavsky, who should be touring the world, saving the best lines in the play for himself, or indeed as the world's greatest stage magician, pulling real as well as metaphorical rabbits out of hats for his delighted audience.

Instead of complaint, however, I merely enquired of Holmes, his plans for unmasking the culprit.

"The Tsar and the Tsarina have invited us to take tea with them today. I expect that our man will be present."

"Then the traitor is a member of the Imperial retinue," I cried.

"Quite so," he replied. "But it was a fact never in doubt." He leaned forward and knocked out his pipe on the firedog. "Now, my dear fellow. My plans for later are cut and dried. What do you say to a little sport? I believe that I can find the billiards rooms so, shall we play one hundred up whilst we wait for the weather to improve?"

Tea was taken in the red drawing room, a particular favourite of the Imperial couple when parted from their children. The room was quite square and not much larger than the sitting room shared by Holmes and myself. The walls were hung with many paintings, mostly of the Tsar's Imperial predecessors and the high windows were draped by velvet curtains of the deepest crimson. The fire, I was glad to see, was piled high with blazing pine logs, with their sharp and clean resinous odour filling the room.

The Tsar and Tsarina were ensconced in large comfortable armchairs either side of the magnificent Adam fireplace and when the servant Yanulov ushered Holmes and myself into the room, the Tsar stood up and waved us to the settee between their chairs. "Thank you, Yanulov," he said in English. "Serve the tea now, if you please."

As I sank into the deep yielding seat, I gazed at my surroundings. How like a typical English afternoon scene, high tea with all the anticipation of sampling the prepared fare. Yanulov appeared by my elbow, he was holding a silver tray. "Will you take your tea black or white, sir," he said in commendable English.

"White with sugar, thank you," I replied.

Later, when all present had been satisfied, the Tsarina temporarily excused herself. She explained that Grand Duchess Sonia was expecting her for a game of bezique.

"You may smoke if you wish, gentlemen," said the Tsar, when the Tsarina had departed. Opening a drawer in the fireside cabinet, he took out a large box. Yanulov as assiduous as ever, opened it for his master and produced a large Havana. Holmes and I, preferring our pipes, refused a cigar. The Tsar relaxed into his chair and blew a smoke ring into the air. Once more I looked around at this very domestic scene and smiled.

"You have not invited Brother Grigory?" said Holmes suddenly.

"No, Mr. Holmes," said the Tsar sharply. "He has displeased me greatly with that ridiculous display last evening. Had we not all been friends, the matter might have proved to be very serious. I have punished him by sending him to Coventry for three days."

I sighed quietly. It was exactly as Holmes had predicted, instead of punishing Brother Grigory for his cupidity, the Tsar had clearly decided to let the matter drop and had determined on the most trivial chastisement.

"Let me tell you about my time in England, gentlemen," said the Tsar. "It was a time when the world seemed mine for the taking, before the burden of Imperial responsibility weighed so heavily upon my shoulders." He sipped his tea then continued. "It was in 1893, when my beloved wife and I were invited to attend the wedding of Prince George, before he became the Prince of Wales." The Tsar chuckled. "I remember as if it was yesterday, the embarrassment of those who mistook us for each other."

There came a sharp knock at the door and Grand Duke Nicholas entered the room, he was quickly followed by the Tsarina, the Grand Duchess Sonia and their retinue. The Duke had convinced the Imperial ladies that it would be agreeable if they would rejoin the party.

The Tsarina, in spite of her lofty position, proved to be quite reserved and reticent, but after a little prompting on the part of the Tsar, she recalled the number of visits they had made to England. One memory in particular made her smile broadly. "It was when my dear husband and I stayed with Queen Victoria at Osborne House in 1894. At first we stopped for a short while in a little cottage in Walton-on-Thames, which was a perfect idyll. Then later we visited her Majesty at home," she turned to the Tsar. "Do you remember, dearest Nicky?"

The Tsar laughed. "Indeed. I remember it most clearly, Alix, particularly as it was when Queen Victoria took off her shoes and stockings and paddled in the sea."

"That is right," the Tsarina said. "And do you remember how one of her shoes floated off into the sea and was never seen again?"

"Yes," said the Tsar. "I also remember that, in 1909, you and I searched the beach in the vain hope that it had somehow floated back again."

The Tsar and Tsarina laughed together, enjoying a shared memory.

Sherlock Holmes, never a man for sentiment, cleared his throat, a little too loudly, I fancy; nevertheless, he obtained the attention he was seeking. He reached into an inside pocket and extracted an envelope. Opening it, he took the sheet of paper within carefully by one of the corners and extracted it. It was the note written by Ulyanov to the Bolsheviks who had kidnapped Hunter Andrews. He held it up for general inspection.

"So this is the communication which has caused you to travel so many miles?" said the Tsarina.

"It is, your Majesty," replied Holmes. "But whilst it is a souvenir of our adventure, it is also a piece of vital evidence, because when Dr. Watson and I return to London, the note will be subjected to rigorous inspection. I am told that because of a new procedure, there is an excellent chance that the fingerprints of the author will be revealed. If so, your Okhrana will be sent a copy of them, so when any felon suspected of being Ulyanov is taken in for questioning, the police will immediately be able to identify him." So saying, Holmes carefully replaced the note in its envelope and returned it to his pocket. He smiled briefly at the assembly. "Very quickly, Ulyanov will discover that for him, there will be no hiding place anywhere in Russia."

The Tsar clapped his hands and laughed. "Excellent, Mr. Holmes. Excellent."

Suddenly a servant was once more standing by my elbow proffering tea.

"It is Orange Pekoe," the Tsar explained. "I always drink some before returning to my work."

Taking the hint that the afternoon's entertainment was virtually at an end, Holmes and I quickly finished our tea and departed to our rooms with a licence to entertain ourselves as best we could.

*****

I had been in bed for some hours, when a sudden unexpected noise dragged me from my slumber. The fire, which had burned so brightly when I had slipped beneath the sheets, by now had burned low and a chill enveloped the room. In the glow of the moonlight, which shone through the partly open curtains, I could see nothing untoward, perhaps it was the sound of the old building settling down for the night that had disturbed me.

Then, just as I had drifted off to sleep once more, another louder noise came from somewhere. I sat up in bed, a door had been opened and closed. I reached out for my jacket and the Vestas in the top pocket and striking one, I looked at my watch hanging on the stand. It was just after three in the morning.

Silently, I slipped from my bed and stole across to the door. Praying that the hinges would not give me away, I gently opened it enough to peer into the sitting room. The fire had died down, but not to the extent where it no longer gave off any light. Then my heart jumped into my mouth, because the outline of a figure was crossing the fire and moving slowly towards the corridor.

Keeping to the shadow of the Persian screen, I reached out for the heavy candlestick I knew to be on the little table by the door to my room. But as my fingers closed around the cold metal, a hand came out of the darkness and grasped me firmly by the wrist. A sharp bitter taste of fear invaded my mouth as I saw the eyes of my unknown companion glittering in the firelight. Then, as a spurt of flame briefly illuminated the room, I recognised my companion to be Sherlock Holmes. His finger was raised to his lips in a gesture of silence. Releasing my hand, he signalled for me to remain quite still and whilst my heart slowly began to return to a more normal beat, we watched as our uninvited visitor opened the door then departed into the night.

"Holmes!" I protested. "Will you tell me exactly what is happening? Why have you let a sneak thief depart unchallenged?"

Holmes lit the table lamp and the room was bathed in light. In the glow, I could see the broad smile on the face of my friend, an event as rare in my experience as snow in July. Quite clearly everything was not as it appeared to be.

He picked up the jacket he had worn earlier from the chair upon which he had draped it and felt in the pockets. After a brief search a small cry of satisfaction escaped his lips. "Excellent," he said. "It is exactly as I had hoped, Watson. The letter from Ulyanov has been taken."

"Taken?" I cried in surprise. "Holmes, what is this all about? Clearly you were expecting a nocturnal visitor. Why on earth did you omit to tell me?"

"My dear fellow, such a petulant face," said Holmes, chuckling. "I do see, however, that I owe you an explanation."

Holmes poured two stiff brandies from the decanter and set me down in a fireside chair, before attacking the fire with a poker. He quickly had a good fire blazing, then he sat down in the chair opposite and began to elucidate.

"No doubt you will recall that earlier this afternoon I exhibited the Ulyanov letter?"

"Indeed, and I have to say, Holmes, that I found it all a little theatrical."

"Possibly, Watson. Possibly," he sighed. "But it was, however, a means to an end. You will also recall our earlier conversation about the Bolshevik infiltrator in the Imperial household?"

"Another of your theatrical devices," I said rather peevishly.

"Well, now. Theatrical or not, my dear fellow, it was the as yet unnamed infiltrator who has come to collect the prize I have so temptingly dangled before him."

"You believed that someone present in the room would recognise the communication, believe all that nonsense about fingerprints and resolve to retrieve it from you?"

"Indeed," he agreed leaning back in his chair and surveying me severely. "And had it not been for the untimely intervention of your good self, Watson, I should not have failed to apprehend him."

My heart became filled with the pang of a mixed emotion. My activities had allowed the miscreant to escape his clutches. On the other hand, however, if Holmes would insist in keeping me in the dark, then he only had myself to blame when on this rare occasion, his plans had played him false. And yet, Holmes appeared to be quite sanguine about it. He slapped me upon the knee and smiled. "It is of little consequence, Watson. Although the fellow does not realise it, the taking of Ulyanov's communication has marked him out as clearly as if he were to be carrying a placard saying, 'I am a thief and a traitor'."

"My dear fellow!" I exclaimed. "How so?"

"I have ensured that because of his activities, our man now has a chemical upon his hands, which under the right conditions will display his guilt to all who are interested to see it," he said. "Even if he has destroyed the letter we shall have sufficient evidence to apprehend him."

Holmes stood up and walked across the room and opened the door to his bedroom. He smiled. "All we shall need is the juice of a lemon, Watson, then we will have him."

*****

It was in the middle of the next morning that Sherlock Holmes and I were booked for a final audience. Holmes had announced over breakfast that we would be departing Tsarskoe Selo that afternoon, he was convinced that he would be able to unmask the traitor and send the Tsar and Tsarina on their journey next day to the Crimea in a more relaxed frame of mind.

The Imperial family had gathered together for the final time, in part to say *bon voyage* to Holmes and myself. As before, Grand Duchess Sonia, Grand Duke Michael and Grand Duke Nicholas were in attendance, only Grand Duke Paul was absent, he had travelled earlier to St. Petersburg to ensure that the Imperial train was prepared for the journey to Lyvadia.

Almost at once, Holmes broached the subject of the Ulyanov letter. At first he was to dismay the assembly with the news that it had been taken by an unknown hand. The Tsar was predictably annoyed by the news. Holmes, however, remained unperturbed. "All is not lost, your Majesty. A final throw of the die has yet to be made."

The Tsar looked doubtfully at Holmes. "I cannot see how you can remain so confident, Mr. Holmes," he said. "If the paper has been taken then the thief has undoubtedly destroyed it and with this destruction comes the inevitable loss of the fingerprints by which we may identify Ulyanov."

A sharp knock at the door interrupted the Tsar's flow of eloquence. The servants had arrived with the morning tea and for the present, conversation was postponed.

A servant offered Holmes milk and sugar, but he declined, asking for lemon instead. I smiled at his request, realising the intent, if not the exact *modus operandi*.

"Excellent, Mr. Holmes," cried Grand Duke Nicholas. "You are taking your tea Russian style."

The servant brought Holmes his tea and waited patiently whilst he squeezed the lemon slice into the beverage. Holmes then dropped the slice into the hand of the servant, then returned to the conversation.

"Now, Mr. Holmes," said the Tsarina. "You must tell us how you intend to unmask the man."

Holmes gazed at the lady through hooded eyes. "He will unmask himself," he replied evenly.

Grand Duke Michael laughed harshly. "Mr. Holmes, I believe that in some quarters you are regarded as little short of a miracle worker, but do you really expect sophisticated and intelligent people to believe such promises? The fellow has clearly ensconced himself within the Imperial household and will be able to fully cover his tracks. You will need more than tricks and sleight of hand to unmask him."

Outraged at this unfair and low slur on the competence of my friend, I made to rise from my seat and protest. A sharp look from Holmes, however, persuaded me that it was an unnecessary enterprise. He said nothing and merely made one of his sharp little smiles. Walking over to the table where the servants were busying themselves, he spoke to Yanulov. "If I might be permitted a little more tea?"

The scene was played out exactly as before. Depositing the slice of lemon into the servant's hand, Holmes took a sip of the tea and pronounced it to be excellent. He looked out of the window and surveyed the view. "This is a splendid place, Tsarskoe Selo. Here a man could want for nothing. It is indeed the same wherever your Majesty goes, even your vehicle of transportation is appointed to the highest possible standards. It is also said, your Majesty, that you are enormously wealthy and I can see for myself that you are handsome, well educated and have a beautiful family, something any man whatever his status might be proud. And yet, in spite of your power, wealth and status, you remain unloved by your people. Indeed, such is the fear of their wrath, that your army commander-in-chief has deployed troops in the concern that trouble in the gold fields of Siberia might spread nation-wide. Is it then any surprise that the Bolsheviks thrive today in Russia?"

I looked at Holmes with blank amazement. It was one thing to speak with such devastating frankness to priests, officials, even Prime Ministers, but this was quite a different matter.

Swiftly my eyes fell upon the face of the Tsar. It was as I had feared, the normal relaxed, even dreamy expression had evaporated. In its place there was a dark foreboding look on his face. "Mr. Holmes," he said, his voice trembling with suppressed anger. "I am unused to being hectored in my own home." He took a deep breath, then his face relaxed into its usual expression. "But I dare say that you mean well." He sighed. "It is true that my people do not love me, but if it is my fate to remain unloved, then so be it."

Sherlock Holmes walked behind the table once more and casually inspected the used tea things. He picked up the silver tray upon which the lemon slices had been deposited and handed it to Yanulov. "But there is much you can do to change things, your Majesty," he said. "Simple alterations may be made, allow direct elections to the Duma, appoint commissioners to the oblasts and charge them with discovering the people's needs and wants. If you try, you will discover that squaring the circle is not as difficult as you might imagine."

The Tsar shook his head. "You mean well, Mr. Holmes, but if the Bolsheviks attempt to overthrow me, they will discover that their fate will be the same now as it was in 1905. Do not underestimate the Okhrana, all they need do is arrest Ulyanov and the whole Bolshevik house of cards will tumble to the ground."

Grand Duke Michael snorted. It was quite clear that he believed that the apprehension of the Bolshevik leader was remote in the extreme.

"Well now," said Holmes. "Perhaps your heart's desire may be closer than you imagine."

The Tsar laughed. "Mr. Holmes, if you can provide evidence which leads to his arrest, then you may have the pick of my personal collection of Fabergé ornaments."

Holmes made no reply, however, he walked behind the servant, who was clearing away the debris of our refreshments. "Here, Yanulov," he said, handing him a cup and saucer apparently overlooked.

Then as the man held out his hand, Holmes grasped his wrist and twisted his arm behind his back. Yanulov gave a sharp cry of pain as Holmes dragged him across the room.

"Mr. Holmes!" cried the Tsarina. "What do you think you are doing?"

"Merely unmasking the man who has been for so long the worm at the heart of the Imperial apple," he said mildly and somewhat poetically, I felt.

"Yanulov?" I asked.

"Indeed." Holmes twisted the arm of the servant and held his right hand up for general inspection. It was smeared with a mauve stain.

"The thief," I murmured.

"Just so," Holmes agreed.

The Tsar jumped to his feet. "Are you convinced that this is the man, Mr. Holmes?"

"Quite convinced."

"Very well ..." The Tsar pulled a bell rope beside the fire and moments later the room door burst open and two of the Imperial bodyguards stood there.

"Jim. David. Please escort Yanulov to the punishment room. I will join you there in a few moments."

Sherlock Holmes released the struggling servant into the hands of the bodyguards and they dragged him struggling and cursing from the room.

The Tsar retook his seat and Holmes did likewise. "Well, Mr. Holmes. Perhaps you can explain exactly how you have managed to pull this particular rabbit out of the hat?"

Holmes surveyed the assembly with hooded eyes. He leaned back into his chair and placed the tips of his long tapering fingers together. "It was a simple matter," he said languidly. "When I discovered that there was an unfriendly spirit at the heart of the Imperial household, it seemed to me that he would have to be of long standing; in order to make best usage of his position it would be necessary for him to be in close contact with the daily household's affairs. I assume, for instance, that his position obliged him to accompany your Majesties from official residence to official residence?"

The Tsar nodded.

"Excellent, then we progress. Clearly in this house, as with most other noble employers, there is no 'not in front of the servants' policy?"

Again the Tsar nodded his assent.

"Then our friend will have overheard virtually all matters you have discussed as a family, including some minor state secrets.

"It follows, therefore, that he would have heard all about the Ulyanov letter, and when I displayed it so openly last evening, he could hardly contain a strong desire to have it back, particularly when I had made it clear that the author's fingerprints were decipherable and could cost him his freedom.

"After I had ensured that all present had properly viewed the letter, I replaced it in my pocket and retired to my room, leaving my coat prominently displayed on the back of an upright chair in our sitting room. If the spy was present, I knew he would make an early attempt to steal the letter, thus accordingly I made every effort possible to ensure the ease of its retrieval.

"There was one factor, however, which our friend could not expect to encounter. A few days ago, I was able to mix a few simple chemicals with the aid of the Tsarevich's chemistry set, then soak the letter in a solution of the compound. Fortunately when the solution dried into the paper, it became quite invisible, but when it came into contact with the skin of anyone who was foolish enough to handle it without firstly taking the precaution of wearing gloves, some of the compound would adhere.

"When friend Yanulov purloined the letter from my jacket pocket, he had to ensure that it was indeed the very communication sent by Ulyanov to his agents. As he did so his hands became covered in the compound and even with prolonged hand washing he became a marked man.

"Today you will have noticed that I took my tea with lemon. Indeed, Grand Duke Nicholas remarked approvingly on my conversion to Russian customs. As Watson has discovered, it was the lemon that was required for the completion of my case. The acid in the juice would change the compound still on the hands of the thief and his identity would be plain for all to see. All that was required of me was to ensure that each of those whom I suspected handled the slices of lemon. It was a task, my dear Grand Duke Michael, I recall you asserting, that was beyond my powers."

"Remarkable," said the Tsar.

"Congratulations, Mr. Holmes," rumbled Grand Duke Nicholas.

Holmes gazed at his audience, his face a veritable picture of self-satisfaction. Then, he held up a hand, apparently he had not quite completed his narration. "There is one thing more," he said. "Your Majesty, for how long has Yanulov been in your employ?"

The Tsar thought for a moment. "I suppose he has been with us for about a year."

"Indeed," said Holmes nodding. "Grand Duke Nicholas, for how long has Ulyanov, the author of this communication, been in exile?"

"Let me see," said the Duke, taking out his pocket memorandum and referring to it. "It was in May last year when the Okhrana had the last report about him." He quickly referred to the notes following. "He was reported to be in Cracow in our Polish territory."

Holmes nodded. "A remarkable coincidence, do you not think?"

The Duke looked puzzled. "I do not quite understand …"

Sherlock Holmes turned his attention to the Tsar. "How is your Majesty at anagrams?"

Holmes felt inside his jacket and took out his pocket book, quickly wrote down two names, then he tore out the sheet of paper and handed it to the Tsar.

The Tsar glanced at the paper for a few seconds, then gave a violent start. "Good Lord. Mr. Holmes, are you certain?"

"Quite certain."

"Then we have in our grasp the very man whom we have been seeking for so long. Excellent, Mr. Holmes."

I was considerably mystified at the warmth of the exchange between the two and I had to wait for several frustrating minutes before the paper Holmes had written upon came into my hands. It was only when I read and digested the contents, I fully understood. The note read thus:

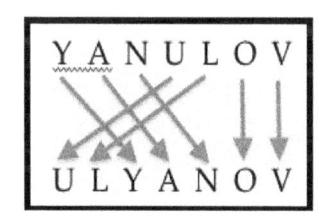

```
Y A N U L O V
U L Y A N O V
```

"Yanulov the servant and Ulyanov the Bolshevik are one and the same," I cried.

Holmes laughed. "Of course they are, my boy."

"For how long have you known?"

"It was a possibility I had suspected for some time," he replied. "Indeed, when I first heard the name Yanulov, I mused on the possibility that it was an anagram of Ulyanov. It was only later when I considered that the best place for a wanted Bolshevik to hide himself away would be at the very heart of the regime which he is seeking to destroy."

"And who would suspect such impudence?"

"Exactly."

Suddenly the air was alive with the sound of gunshots. There were three, evenly spaced coming from somewhere within the palace walls. All present simply sprang from their seats, but Holmes and Grand Duke Nicholas were quickest. The Duke instructed the remaining servants to protect the Imperial family and Holmes called for my assistance. "Watson. Are you carrying your revolver?"

Momentarily I cursed myself for not having the foresight to be armed and I was forced to reply in the negative.

"No matter, Mr. Holmes," said Grand Duke Nicholas. "If the guards were not themselves responsible for the shots, they will have heard them and acted accordingly."

Making light of his years, the Duke ran along the corridor, well in advance of Holmes and myself.

"This can only be the work of Ulyanov," Holmes cried. "Why did I not search him to see if he was armed?"

We turned the corner and arrived at the head of the grand staircase. Grand Duke Nicholas was quickly issuing orders to the various bodyguards who were in evidence. There was a general hubbub as we reached the foot of the stairs, the activity reminded me of an ants's nest that had been disturbed by a careless boot. A number of Cossacks were standing over a prostrate figure, a quick glance showed him to be Jim Hercules. He was bleeding quite profusely from what seemed to be a nasty wound to his head.

"Jim," I said kneeling down by his side. "What happened?"

"It was Yanulov," he said weakly. "We didn't see he was packing a gun until it was too late. David and me was marching him off to the lock-up like the boss said, when he pulled out this silver gun and pointed it at us. Like a fool ah tried to grab it off him. It went off in the struggle and here ah am."

I quickly inspected his dark curly head. To my great relief, I discovered that the wound, although leaking a great deal of blood, was not as bad as I had first feared.

"Think Ah'll live, Dr. Watson?" he asked.

"I expect so," I replied smiling. "After a little remedial treatment, you will be fine."

Abruptly from the rear of the palace, there came a chorus of shouts and cries followed by a number of gunshots. Then, into the hall a party of Cossacks came running. At the sight of Grand Duke Nicholas they stopped abruptly and asked for orders. Quickly, however, the duke sent them on their way.

The main doors were thrown open and the Cossacks spread out into the afternoon sunshine. Suddenly there came the roar of a motorcar engine and the crunch and squeal of tyres on gravel. Leaving Jim in the hands of the newly arrived Dr. Deverenko, I followed the veritable stream of armed men out into the open air. Seeing Holmes, I tugged at his sleeve. "My dear fellow. What is happening?"

"It is Ulyanov," he said sharply. "He has managed to steal one of the Tsar's motorcars."

As he spoke, a silver and black Rolls Royce sped into view from the direction of the Catherine Palace. It was going at high speed and as the motorcar flashed past us, I could see the balding figure of Ulyanov behind the wheel, clearly, in his haste, he had taken a wrong turn and was doubling back towards the main entrance to Tsarskoe Selo.

Grand Duke Nicholas barked out an order and those in the company of Cossacks who were armed fired a fusillade of shots at the swiftly retreating vehicle. Yet, in spite of the number of hits, the motorcar raced on and I have to admit my profound admiration for the courage and resourcefulness of Ulyanov.

"He is escaping, Watson," cried Holmes. "We can only hope that the main gates hold him."

A second motorcar appeared, a Humber, I believe. Again I recognised the driver. It was Mr. Littov, Grand Duke Nicholas's aide. The Duke threw open a passenger door. "Quickly, Mr. Holmes," he cried. "We may yet apprehend the fellow."

Holmes and I swiftly followed the Duke into the motorcar and we were thrown roughly into our seats by the acceleration as Littov drove off in hot pursuit of our quarry. As I looked out on the pleasure grounds, I could see six or seven riders galloping after our vehicle.

Then at last we turned into the final strait. I could see the entrance to the Tsar's village. Both gates were wide open and one was hanging drunkenly from one hinge. Clearly our man had not been hindered in the least by this barrier.

Grand Duke Nicholas glanced at the scene and uttered a muted oath. "Stop the car," he ordered. "Ulyanov has escaped us and there is no way in which we may tell the direction he has taken."

Our motorcar screeched to a halt. Holmes, however, was not so easily discouraged. He jumped out into the roadway and crouched down upon his haunches and gazed at the scene before him. Quickly he examined the gates then momentarily, he threw himself to the ground. Jumping to his feet once more, he signalled to Littov that he should re-start the engine.

As the vehicle drew level with him, Holmes thrust his head through the open window.

"He has taken the St. Petersburg road," he said. "There are large amounts of silver paint on the left hand gate, traces of rubber on the roadway and a large black rubber mark on the kerbstone on the left."

"Excellent, Mr. Holmes," said the Duke firmly, "Littov and I will follow Ulyanov. If Dr. Watson and yourself would care to return to the palace and telephone ahead, we may yet outmanoeuvre him."

As the Duke's motorcar disappeared into the distance. I smiled at Holmes and mused quietly at the long walk before us.

"Come along, old fellow," I said. "If we hurry, we may even reach the palace before Ulyanov gets to St. Petersburg."

Nicholas II and the Prince of Wales,
later King George V, at Cowes, 1909

Epilogue

It was late afternoon and the sun was already sinking behind the hills. Sherlock Holmes and I were on the road between St. Petersburg and the port of the Peterhof some thirty miles to the north west, where a steamer from the imperial flotilla had been readied to carry Holmes and myself to Stockholm on the first leg of our journey home.

After a short speech stocked with the usual fund of thanks and regrets, the Tsar had presented Holmes and myself with a cigarette case each. They were made of gold with enamelled fascias of dark Prussian blue with the flags of Imperial Russia and of St. George. Set into the enamel and like glittering stars, were two small diamonds.

In a breach of the usual protocol, the Tsar stepped forward and furiously hugged Sherlock Holmes. "Thank you, Mr. Holmes," he said. "You have done as much for Russia as any native of the motherland."

Releasing Holmes the Tsar then held me in a bear hug. "Dr. Watson. You have also proved to be a steadfast friend. I salute you."

Grand Duke Nicholas, who had recently returned from St. Petersburg, had a word for me also.

"My dear Doctor. It has been a particular pleasure for me to make your acquaintance. My only regret is that we have had insufficient time to explore our shared interest in military history. I fear that events may intervene which will prevent us from ever meeting again."

I looked across the carriage at the figure hunched in the corner. If anything he seemed to be deeper in thought than I. "A penny for your thoughts, old man?" I said.

Holmes surfaced from his ocean of introspection. "I am not even sure that my thoughts are worth as much as a penny," he muttered.

"Never mind, Holmes," I said. "I am quite prepared to be overcharged."

"My record at Tsarskoe Selo has been less than perfect, Watson. I have erred too many times."

"My dear fellow," I cried. "How so?"

Holmes leaned forward and pulled down the window slightly and allowed the rushing air to suck out his cigarette. "I have made three serious errors. One, I allowed Shukin and his associates to be taken to the Peter and Paul fortress by the Okhrana without first interrogating them myself. Two, I failed to foresee the intervention of Brother Grigory when I knew full well of the intimate relationship that existed between the Tsar, Tsarina and himself. Three, I made the simple mistake, failing to search Ulyanov before having him removed into custody." He sighed. "Perhaps my age has finally caught up with me and my powers are deserting me also."

"Nonsense, Holmes," I cried. "You judge yourself too harshly. Do not forget that you are a stranger in a strange land. I have no doubt any small errors made in Russia would not be replicated under normal circumstances."

Holmes smiled and patted me gently on the arm. "Good old Watson, loyal to the last. It is unfortunate, but I see the truth with pellucid clarity. The moving finger having writ moves on; that is what I must do."

I shook my head in disbelief at what I was hearing. "But on this journey you have achieved so much. You have saved the reputation of Miss Alice Ward; without your intervention I have not the slightest doubt that she would even now be languishing in an Italian prison. You have unmasked a murderer in Bucharest. You have outwitted bandits. You have saved the Tsar from the Bolsheviks. Most of all, Holmes, you have saved the life of your brother, Mycroft. If that is not enough to satisfy you, I do not know what is?"

Holmes shook his head. "That may be so, Watson. But small errors lead inevitably to big errors. Fortune will not always favour me. It is my wish to retire into oblivion before my faults find me out."

"But you have much to offer, Holmes. As long as you handle a case successfully, your clients will hardly know if you have made a mistake along the way."

"Ah, Watson. The fact is that *I* will know."

Our carriage rattled through the dockyard gates and very soon we found ourselves boarding the steamer.

After Holmes and I had been shown our cabins and we had unpacked our meagre belongings, we took a turn on deck. The boat had slipped her moorings and was making a frothy white wake in the velvet sea below. For the present there was silence between us, each man deep in his own thoughts. At last it was Sherlock Holmes who spoke. "It will mean quite a reception when we get home, my boy. Word of our adventure will have spread throughout the land. Mrs. Andrews will have broadcast the safe return of her husband and the newspapers will have been all too ready to take up the story."

"Indeed," I agreed. "There will be important people to meet. Lord Falmouth and Sir Arthur Richardson, not to mention our sailor friend, Tom Hockney. Or indeed, Chief Inspector Lestrade."

Holmes laughed. "Poor Lestrade. He was the unwilling rear of our pantomime donkey and will be furious to discover how neatly we have deceived him."

I chuckled at the thought of Lestrade's discomfiture. It also occurred to me that whilst in Sussex, Holmes had alluded to the possible poisoning of the Tsar and Tsarina. Indeed, he had virtually confirmed as much in Tsarskoe Selo. But he had proved to be unforthcoming on the matter ever since. Now whilst the idea was fresh in my mind, I resolved to get a definitive answer.

"It was lead poisoning without any doubt." Holmes agreed. "My chemical analysis of the hair samples taken from the Tsar and Tsarina showed there had been considerable absorption."

"You have not explained how the dosage was administered. All that we can assume is that it was undoubtedly given over a long period, so that there were no violent effects, merely a slow decline in their health."

"Just so."

"But who was the poisoner? Was it Ulyanov, or does it still remain a mystery?"

"Oh, there is no mystery, Watson," he said airily. "Likewise there is no poisoner."

"I do not understand."

"The compound was not introduced, it was present in the water supply. My experimentation on several samples proved convincing. By drinking the water at Tsarskoe Selo, the Imperial family is slowly poisoning itself."

"Good heavens."

"Prior to our departure, I informed the Tsar and explained that unless a new supply for the Tsar's village is provided, then the health of the Imperial family will continue to deteriorate."

"Well, you have done what you can," I said.

"Unfortunately, the Tsar seems to have considerable trouble with following advice. Let us hope that he will at least do something about his drinking water, if not his empire."

The night was becoming decidedly cold and there was the matter of supper to be considered. Holmes and I walked down the steps to the little cabin which was to be our mess for the next few days. Before the meal was served, we sipped a small *aperitif*.

"Holmes!"

"Yes, my dear fellow?"

"Have you discovered bee-keeping to be a particularly difficult pastime?"

"It can be time consuming, depending upon the season. But why do you ask?"

"I have been thinking that I would like to learn the art; if you would care to teach it to me."

"My dear fellow, it would be a pleasure. Let us get this business behind us, Watson, then we may retire to Sussex and I shall begin your lessons."

I took another sip of my drink, then raised the glass in a salute. "Capital, Holmes," I said warmly. "Capital."

"With five volumes you could fill that gap on that second shelf."
(Sherlock Holmes, *The Empty House*)

So why not complete your collection of murder mysteries from Baker Street Studios? Available from all good bookshops, or direct from the publisher. To see full details of all our publications, range of audio books, and special offers visit www.crime4u.com where you can also join our mailing list.

IN THE DEAD OF WINTER
SHERLOCK HOLMES AND DR. CRIPPEN
SHERLOCK HOLMES AND THE ABBEY SCHOOL MYSTERY
SHERLOCK HOLMES AND THE ADLER PAPERS
SHERLOCK HOLMES AND THE BAKER STREET DOZEN
SHERLOCK HOLMES AND THE BOULEVARD ASSASSIN
SHERLOCK HOLMES AND THE CASE OF THE HISSING SHAFT
SHERLOCK HOLMES AND THE CHARLIE CHAPLIN AFFAIR
SHERLOCK HOLMES AND THE CHILFORD RIPPER
SHERLOCK HOLMES AND THE CHINESE JUNK AFFAIR
SHERLOCK HOLMES AND THE CIRCUS OF FEAR
SHERLOCK HOLMES AND THE DISAPPEARING PRINCE
SHERLOCK HOLMES AND THE DISGRACED INSPECTOR
SHERLOCK HOLMES AND THE EGYPTIAN HALL ADVENTURE
SHERLOCK HOLMES AND THE FRIGHTENED CHAMBERMAID
SHERLOCK HOLMES AND THE FRIGHTENED GOLFER
SHERLOCK HOLMES AND THE GIANT'S HAND
SHERLOCK HOLMES AND THE GREYFRIARS SCHOOL MYSTERY
SHERLOCK HOLMES AND THE HAMMERFORD WILL
SHERLOCK HOLMES AND THE HILLDROP CRESCENT MYSTERY
SHERLOCK HOLMES AND THE HOLBORN EMPORIUM
SHERLOCK HOLMES AND THE HOUDINI BIRTHRIGHT
SHERLOCK HOLMES AND THE LONG ACRE VAMPIRE
SHERLOCK HOLMES AND THE MAN WHO LOST HIMSELF
SHERLOCK HOLMES AND THE MORPHINE GAMBIT
SHERLOCK HOLMES AND THE SANDRINGHAM HOUSE MYSTERY
SHERLOCK HOLMES AND THE SECRET MISSION
SHERLOCK HOLMES AND THE SECRET SEVEN
SHERLOCK HOLMES AND THE TANDRIDGE HALL MYSTERY
SHERLOCK HOLMES AND THE TELEPHONE MURDER MYSTERY
SHERLOCK HOLMES AND THE THEATRE OF DEATH
SHERLOCK HOLMES AND THE THREE POISONED PAWNS
SHERLOCK HOLMES AND THE TITANIC TRAGEDY
SHERLOCK HOLMES AND THE TOMB OF TERROR
SHERLOCK HOLMES AND THE YULE-TIDE MYSTERY
SHERLOCK HOLMES: A DUEL WITH THE DEVIL
SHERLOCK HOLMES AT THE RAFFLES HOTEL
SHERLOCK HOLMES AT THE VARIETIES
SHERLOCK HOLMES ON THE WESTERN FRONT
SHERLOCK HOLMES: THE GHOST OF BAKER STREET
SPECIAL COMMISSION
THE ADVENTURE OF THE SPANISH DRUMS
THE CASE OF THE MISSING STRADIVARIUS
THE ELEMENTARY CASES OF SHERLOCK HOLMES
THE TORMENT OF SHERLOCK HOLMES
THE TRAVELS OF SHERLOCK HOLMES
WATSON'S LAST CASE

Baker Street Studios Limited, Endeavour House, 170 Woodland Road, Sawston, Cambridge CB22 3DX